A stable, happy woman named Sandy Hunter one morning doesn't show up for work. She is seen on security cameras entering the Bennington Hotel from the parking garage. She is then seen using a key card to get into a hotel room. No way of knowing how she got the card since she did not go to the front desk to get it.

Yet she had it.

She vanished the moment she entered the room and the door closed.

No security coverage showed anyone going or coming from the room except maid service earlier in the morning three hours before she arrived.

After Sandy Hunter, the next time that door was opened was when a detective named Carl Bower from the University Station showed up at the door with a manager. They opened the door and there was no sign the woman had been in the room.

It was impossible, but Sandy Hunter never left the building.

She vanished from a locked room without a trace.

When Pickett finished reading the report, she looked up at Robin who was sitting staring off into space.

The Cold Poker Gang was supposed to solve cold cases, but this one was so cold, it had ice caked on it.

Layers and layers of ice.

ALSO BY DEAN WESLEY SMITH

Cold Poker Gang Mysteries:

Kill Game

Cold Call

Calling Dead

Bad Beat

Dead Hand

Freezeout

Ace High

Burn Card

Heads Up

Ring Game

Bottom Pair

Doc Hill Thrillers:

Dead Money

"The Road Back"

FREEZEOUT

A Cold Poker Gang Mystery

DEAN WESLEY SMITH

WMG PUBLISHING

Freezeout

Copyright © 2021 by Dean Wesley Smith

All rights reserved

First published in *Smith's Monthly* #34, WMG Publishing, July 2016
Published by WMG Publishing
Cover and layout copyright © 2021 by WMG Publishing
Cover design by Allyson Longueira/WMG Publishing
Cover art copyright © Shacil/Depositphotos
ISBN-13: 978-1-56146-773-0
ISBN-10: 1-56146-773-1

FREEZEOUT

Freezeout:

In poker the most common form of a tournament. Players are eliminated until there is only one player left with all the other player's chips.

PART ONE

The Game Starts

PROLOGUE

March 3rd, 2002
Las Vegas, Nevada

Sandy Hunter kissed her husband Rich goodbye in the modern kitchen of their apartment four blocks from Las Vegas University campus. Everything seemed perfectly normal. The morning sun through the kitchen window promised a beautiful spring day and that evening they had date night planned, with a wonderful dinner at their favorite sushi place.

Sandy stood five-two on a good day and looked much taller because she always wore heels, slimming black slacks, and had her medium-length brown hair pulled up on the top of her head. At twenty-four, she was just finishing her second master's degree in business. She worked part time at a securities firm and to everyone around her she appeared to be happy.

She and Rich had many plans for the future.

Rich still had a year to go on his second master's in history and was working at the university. He hoped to eventually become a professor there after a number of years.

He was short at five-five and Sandy often looked taller, something he didn't mind in the slightest. Unlike her, he didn't much care about his height one way or another.

Sandy told Rich she would be home to change clothes before dinner, then went down the three flights of stairs and got into their new Toyota two-door.

Security cameras showed that she pulled out of the apartment complex parking lot, turning toward Las Vegas Boulevard. In normal traffic, it would take her fifteen minutes to get to her office off Charleston. The morning's traffic was normal, as far as the radio said.

She had a meeting in forty-five minutes and had told Rich she wanted to go early to prepare. She had told her co-worker the same thing and they planned on meeting over coffee and Danish rolls thirty minutes ahead of the meeting.

She never arrived at work.

Just before the meeting started her co-worker called Rich to see if Sandy was sick or had forgotten the meeting. Both Rich and the co-worker were instantly worried that Sandy had gotten into a wreck.

After three hours of waiting and calling hospitals and no word, Rich finally called the police. They could do nothing, but a friendly detective listened to Rich and believed him and then called Sandy's office to confirm. Clearly something had happened to Sandy, so the police put out a notice to watch for Sandy's car.

At seven in the evening, Sandy's car was found parked in the Bennington Hotel and Casino underground parking lot just off the Strip. The hotel security cam showed Sandy pulling into the lot seven minutes after she left home, locking her car, and walking calmly into the hotel.

She seemed to know where she was going and was in no hurry.

She went to an elevator, and got off on the eleventh floor. She used a key card she pulled from her small clutch purse to open the door to a room halfway down the hallway.

The room was reserved in the name of Rich Hunter, Sandy's husband, and paid for with his credit card.

Rich swore he knew nothing about it and a check of their financial records showed that was the only time such a charge had been made on either of their cards.

Sandy's behavior was very, very unusual, to say the least. Yet she seemed to be acting normally.

Almost as if she did this every day.

At two in the morning, when the police knocked on the hotel room door, no one answered and the room was empty.

The security cameras showed that no one had left that room after Sandy entered.

And no one had gone in ahead of her either.

The room had been reserved online.

Sandy had left no fingerprints in the room, but the prints from the previous couple who had stayed there were everywhere. Nothing had been wiped down or cleaned beyond the normal maid service.

There were no leads and her missing person's case went quickly cold, with only her husband trying to find out what happened to his wife.

No one had any idea why Sandy Hunter vanished.

Or how a person could simply vanish from a major Las Vegas hotel room without a trace.

CHAPTER ONE

November 16th, 2016
Las Vegas, Nevada

Retired Las Vegas Detective Debra Pickett stood sipping a cup of black coffee, without cream, in the kitchen of her penthouse condo in the Ogden in downtown Las Vegas.

Outside her windows, she could tell the late fall day was shaping up to be another beautiful day. The forecast said the high temperature today would be around seventy.

Perfect. She loved the Vegas spring and fall weather. Comfortable during the day, cool at night.

She stood five-feet-four and had brown hair that she kept short and styled because it was just a bunch easier to deal with every day.

She had on jeans, a cotton blouse, and a light sweater. She had her badge in a holder on her belt covered by her sweater and her service gun in a holster under her arm. She would hide that with a light-brown jacket when she went out.

She and Retired Detective Ben "Sarge" Carson were headed for their normal morning walk along Fremont Street to the Golden Nugget buffet for breakfast. He owned the penthouse condo beside hers. And she had spent the night there, as was becoming wonderfully normal.

Sometimes he stayed with her, but she liked his place even better than her wonderful condo, if that was possible, so the last few weeks they had spent every night in his condo.

She had a fresh cup of coffee sitting on the counter beside her, waiting for him to finish dressing and come over to get her. She had gotten out of the shower first and rousted his handsome body out of bed.

Sarge had thick gray hair and for sixty was in the best shape of any man she had ever seen or been with. Even when she was younger.

On the floor at her feet, a young black and white kitten she affectionately referred to as Nose worked on her morning treat. Nose stayed the night with her at Sarge's place, sometimes sleeping on the bed with them, sometimes running through the condo playing with his two kittens, Pete and Ree. Ree was short for Repeat.

Both his cats were orange tabbies and they looked a lot alike. He had started from the moment he picked them up at the pound calling them Pete and Repeat until he thought of better names. She couldn't save them from the original names no matter how many names she suggested, so at least they had shortened the little one's name to Ree.

And Nose hadn't been her cat's name to start with either. She had called her Cleo, but she had the cutest little white button nose and sometime during the first week after they got the cats, Nose stuck that white button nose into a place it shouldn't be during a human sexual moment.

It seemed the nose was cold and wet and made Sarge shout and then laugh and from that moment onward the cat was stuck with Nose as a name.

Last night, at the Cold Poker Gang poker game, she and Sarge and Pickett's partner Retired Detective Robin Sprague had gotten a new case to work on.

At this point, there were fourteen retired detectives in the Cold Poker Gang, but only about ten showed up for the game on any given Tuesday. She and Sarge and Robin had decided they wouldn't miss a night, they loved it that much.

Before the tunnel case last month, Pickett and Robin had been partners. All through their detective years and afterwards they had been partners and Pickett could never imagine that changing. But with the tunnel case and meeting Sarge, he had become the third member of their team

All three of them loved working the cold cases and working together. Before they retired, none of them seemed to have enough time for many cold cases. That's why the Las Vegas police chief had given the Cold Poker Gang special status to work on cold cases. They could all still carry their guns and their badges. They just didn't get paid.

Having an unpaid group of experienced detectives volunteering to work cold cases freed up the on-duty detectives to do the more pressing work and allowed Las Vegas to now have one of the top-rated levels of closing cold cases in the entire country.

Besides that, no member of the gang had to do any paperwork. And none of them wanted the credit, so they often gave the credit to the working detectives, which kept the working detectives on the side of the Cold Poker Gang as well.

Pickett considered all this the best of both worlds. She could work at her own pace, do the job she still loved, and not have to do paperwork.

She had retired and gone to police heaven, or as Sarge liked to say, "a police fantasy world."

She liked the fantasy, especially working with Robin and now the man she was falling completely in love with.

This week, Retired Detective Andor Williams, the Cold Poker Gang's official contact with the chief of police, had given the three of them a cold case disappearance from March 2002. Pickett remembered something about it being one of the stranger cases she had heard about, but it had been a University Station case and Sarge remembered more about it since that had been where he was based at the time.

Normally, after a Cold Poker Gang meeting, she and Robin and now Sarge went out for dinner to discuss the case, but Robin had a late dinner party she had to go to with her husband, Will, and had to leave the game early. So Sarge and Pickett had promised her they wouldn't even look at the case until they met her at breakfast this morning.

So it was going to be a fun morning. New cases always excited Pickett.

Nose was finished with her morning treat, so Pickett picked up the dish and washed it off, then picked up the kitten and scratched her ears until she purred.

A new case to solve, a new kitten to pet, and a wonderful man in her life. Just didn't get much better.

CHAPTER TWO

November 16th, 2016
Las Vegas, Nevada

Retired Las Vegas Detective Ben "Sarge" Carson finished dressing and made sure that both of his cats had eaten some of their morning treats. They had and were now safely in his living room stretched out on the floor in the sun.

He had really come to love those two and Pickett's cat as well. Wonderful personalities that filled what had been a large, empty condo. Of course, having Pickett in and out and staying over every night made this place feel like a home, of that there was no doubt.

He had dressed in his normal jeans and dress shirt. He kept his badge where it always had been, on his belt on his right hip and his gun in a carry holster under his arm.

For a few years after retiring he hadn't had his badge or his gun, but now that he was back with the Cold Poker Gang, it felt like he was again fully dressed. His entire identity was being a detective and he loved the fact that he didn't have to change that identity now that he was retired.

He put on a light jacket to cover the gun and the badge and then told the two kittens to behave. As cats do, they didn't even notice he was leaving as he went out into the penthouse foyer and then into Pickett's condo. The building had three penthouse condos. His was the largest, with an upstairs area that gave him almost a three hundred degree view of the city and the surrounding hills around Las Vegas.

After he had discovered that Pickett lived next door to him, he had looked into who owned the third one. It was owned by an older couple in Boise who only came to Las Vegas twice a year. The best kind of neighbor.

Pickett had gotten the money for her condo when her husband had a midlife crisis and left for Los Angeles with his thirty-year-old secretary. Sarge had gotten the money for his condo as just a tiny part of his inheritance when his father died four years ago. For retired detectives, they both lived in style. But except for the condos, you could never tell they both had money.

Pickett was holding her cat Nose when he came in. She smiled at him and nodded to the cup of coffee waiting for him on the counter. This was part of their routine that had developed in just a few weeks of knowing each other. She made them coffee in her place and then they walked the four blocks up to the Golden Nugget buffet for breakfast.

He liked the routine a great deal.

He scratched Nose's ears, then leaned against the counter and sipped his coffee. On the counter behind him was the gray folder with the details about their new case.

"You didn't peek at it, did you?" he asked, smiling at Pickett.

"I wanted to, but nope," she said, putting Nose on the

ground. Nose stretched and then headed for the tan cloth couch in the living room area to stretch out in the sun.

"I'm kind of excited about this one," he said.

And he was. He remembered it being a real puzzle from his days on the force when it came up. He hadn't caught the case, but the two detectives who had been assigned the case wanted to bang their heads against a wall at times.

"What do you remember about it?" she asked.

"Sort of a locked room mystery," he said. "I remember a woman who had no business in a major hotel going into the room and never coming out. No sign of her ever being in the room was ever found. Or something like that."

Pickett smiled and looked at the folder. "Robin would kill us if we opened it without her."

Sarge laughed. Robin Sprague had been Pickett's partner for years on the force. They were known as two of the best detectives ever. Robin was married to Will Sprague who owned and ran the city's biggest private protection firm. Robin was an expert on computers and she also had all of Will's people to back her up when needed. And on some cases they really needed the computer work. The three of them were lucky to have that kind of power at their disposal, that was for sure.

When on the regular force, Pickett had liked to do the legwork while Robin did the computer work. Sarge joining them had just given Pickett some company and cover when out knocking on doors and interviewing people. That was how he had done things as well.

He downed the rest of his coffee and rinsed out his cup in the sink, then turned to Pickett. "Let's get to breakfast before one of us opens that file."

Pickett rinsed out her cup and picked up the file. "How

come I feel like a kid at Christmas about ready to open a present?"

"Because we're both warped, that's why," Sarge said, kissing her lightly and then helping her on with her jacket.

Now, walking down the street, they would look like a younger retired couple out for a walk. And Sarge liked the fact that they were a couple a great deal.

CHAPTER THREE

November 16th, 2016
Las Vegas, Nevada

Pickett enjoyed the morning walk in the cool air. It made her feel alive and being alive and happy at the age of sixty-one would not have been something she would have bet would happen ten years earlier.

And walking with Sarge just made it all the better. Their strides seemed to match and she found she laughed a lot while with him.

At the top of the escalator going into the Golden Nugget buffet, she could see Robin already seated and eating at their favorite morning table.

The buffet was separated from the escalator area by a wall of plants and fake windows. The dining area was huge with at least seventy or more tables in three sections. Everything was decorated in brown and brass tones. Not gaudy like some restaurants in Vegas. Pickett thought it was comfortable, actually.

And the smell of ham and omelets made her instantly hungry.

It was her turn to pay and she did, then headed for Robin who looked up and smiled.

Robin had been her best friend for longer than Pickett wanted to think about.

Robin was solid, with square shoulders that showed all the time that she spent in a pool exercising. She had short, silver-gray hair and always wore a baseball cap that was now sitting on a chair beside her. She had on her dark windbreaker that Pickett knew concealed her gun and badge.

Robin was the smartest woman Pickett knew. But what she loved about Robin was that she didn't show the fantastic intelligence unless needed and never flaunted the fact.

Pickett dropped the file on the table near Robin. "No, we did not look, but you can while we get something to eat."

"Oh, fun," Robin said, pulling the file toward her.

Sarge laughed. "As I said, we're all strange."

"And that's news how?" Robin asked, smiling at them.

Ten minutes later Pickett had her slice of ham, scrambled eggs, and orange juice and was back at the table sitting across from Robin. Sarge was waiting for an omelet to be made. He usually had an omelet and a small waffle and orange juice.

They both had another cup of black coffee waiting for them at the table that Robin had signaled the waitress to bring.

Robin looked like she was about halfway through the report and her food was going untouched.

"Better eat," Pickett said.

"Wait until you read this," Robin said, surfacing and taking another bite of her scrambled eggs. "It's going to be damned impossible unless we get a really lucky break."

"Oh, great, one of those," Pickett said.

Actually, that excited her. Challenges were frustrating, sure, but great fun now that their entire careers didn't depend on solving the case.

"This case was cold from moment one," Robin said, shaking her head.

"What's Will up to?" Pickett asked, changing the subject off the case until Sarge got there.

"He and his people have a big convention to help protect some special guests," Robin said, shrugging. "But it's going well so he's been home every evening this last week."

"Can your marriage stand that?" Pickett asked, laughing. She knew that Will and Robin's marriage was about as strong as it came.

"Thank god for this case," Robin said, patting the paper in front of her. "Just what the marriage counselor ordered."

At that moment Sarge joined them and Robin had to get an update on the kittens. A detailed update, which allowed all three of them to get through most of the first round of their breakfasts.

Then Robin handed the first five pages of the report to Pickett and went back to reading.

Pickett read the first page and slid it to Sarge.

As Robin said, this case had been cold from the start.

A stable, happy woman named Sandy Hunter one morning doesn't show up for work. She is seen on security cameras entering the Bennington Hotel from the parking garage. She is then seen using a key card to get into a hotel room. No way of knowing how she got the card since she did not go to the front desk to get it.

Yet she had it.

She vanished the moment she entered the room and the door closed.

No security coverage showed anyone going or coming from the room except maid service earlier in the morning three hours before she arrived.

After Sandy Hunter, the next time that door was opened was when a detective named Carl Bower from the University Station showed up at the door with a manager. They opened the door and there was no sign the woman had been in the room.

The room was checked for blood and fingerprints and everything came up negative. And no way she could have gone out a window. The room was on the seventh floor and there was no ledge outside the window and the window had a secure feature on it that wouldn't allow it to open very wide.

Security showed Sandy Hunter clearly going into that room.

Every minute of every security footage from every camera of the hotel was scanned looking for her after that. No security tapes were tampered with either. Police and security checked and double-checked that.

It was impossible, but Sandy Hunter never left the building.

She vanished from a locked room without a trace.

When Pickett finished reading the report, she looked up at Robin who was sitting staring off into space.

They were supposed to solve cold cases, but this one was so cold, it had ice caked on it.

Layers and layers of ice.

CHAPTER FOUR

November 16th, 2016
Las Vegas, Nevada

Sarge was the last one to finish reading the report. When he did, he sat back, feeling sort of stunned. Around them the normal sounds of the buffet went on. People talking, a group laughing, and plates and silverware clattering. He loved this place. And he loved the food even more.

He remembered Detective Bower and his partner going round and round about this case. In the file it detailed out everything about Rich Hunter, the husband, Sandy's job, and Rich's family. They got Sandy's email files from both home and work.

They came up with a big fat nothing.

There was no reason that Sandy Hunter, on her way to work for an important meeting, would stop at a hotel, use a key card no one knows how she got, and go into a room simply to vanish into thin air. No signs she was having an affair, no signs that she was unhappy in her marriage or her job.

And no signs at all of her in the fourteen years since she vanished.

"So what the hell happened to her?" Sarge asked, looking up at Pickett and then at Robin.

"I bet dead," Robin said. "But damned if I know why or how."

"Maybe kidnapped for sex trade," Pickett said. "She was good-looking enough from the pictures in the file. But how, no idea."

Sarge nodded. "I can see why Bower banged his head against the wall on this one."

"You know Bower?" Pickett asked.

Sarge nodded. "Nice guy, lost his partner about a year after this and decided to stay at a desk until retirement. Gained a lot of weight I hear. Retiring next year."

Robin pulled out a notebook and so did Pickett. Sarge took his from his inside jacket pocket. He used a small flip-page notebook, Pickett used a similar style with a stiffer cover, and Robin had a full spiral-bound notebook.

"So you two get to talk with Bower, see if there's more that's not in the report," Robin said.

Sarge nodded, but he doubted there would be. Bower had been one of the most organized detectives Sarge had ever met, which is why Bower could leave the streets without a problem. He liked the paperwork and every report he ever did was complete.

But Bower might have an opinion and that would be worth the time to talk.

Pickett glanced at Sarge, then turned to Robin. "Why do I have a hunch this isn't an isolated incident?"

"Just one that was caught quickly," Sarge said nodding. "If the police hadn't been ahead of normal procedure on this, someone would have already checked into that room the next day."

"I'll see what I can come up with about people vanishing out of hotel rooms," Robin said, making notes. "But we all know the hotels are extremely private about this sort of thing. Hell, if someone dies in one of their top suites, they move the body so as to not lose the room rental."

Sarge nodded and managed not to smile at how angry Robin sounded about that. Clearly she and Pickett had run into that a few times over the years. Every Las Vegas detective had.

"So we find and talk with the husband and the coworkers," Pickett said, taking the names and old contact information from the file and writing it in her notebook.

"Robin," Sarge asked, "would it be possible to track missing person cases through the police files with references to last time seen in a hotel? Just general."

"There will be a lot of those," Robin said, nodding and writing. "But we can figure out ways to narrow it down later. See if we have a pattern."

Sarge nodded. This was going to be the best they could do. A lot of this was going to be going back over ground already covered by Bower. But just maybe, with a little time, they might find something different.

Maybe.

He didn't hold out much hope on this case. On the small bar in Lott and Julia's basement where the Cold Poker Gang met and played cards once a week, there were four files. All still unsolved.

Sarge bet this one would be the fifth.

CHAPTER FIVE

November 16th, 2016
Las Vegas, Nevada

Pickett liked Detective Bower almost instantly. He had his own office that looked out over a parking lot, which in Vegas was a normal view. His office was fairly large and clean and organized. He had family pictures of his wife, kids, and grandkids hanging on the wall.

He was a heavyset man as Sarge had said, going toward round. But his smile reached his dark eyes and he had a laugh that made people around him want to laugh along. He had on a white dress shirt and no tie and had his suit jacket hanging on a tree-stand near the door.

Pickett would have never figured him for a detective. More like an accountant.

Sarge introduced her and Bower and Sarge exchanged a few old laughs, then Bower indicated they should take a seat in front of his metal desk and he went around behind it and settled into an oversized leather chair that clearly wasn't department issue, but fit his large frame.

"So you two working a cold case for the Cold Poker Gang, huh?" Bower asked, smiling.

"We are," Sarge said.

"If I wasn't going to be so happy to get out of this job next year, I might think about joining the gang. That would be if they needed someone to do some behind the scenes stuff. Not much good out on the streets these days."

He laughed and patted his rounded stomach barely held in by his white dress shirt.

"The gang can use all the help it can get," Sarge said. "In all ways."

Pickett just nodded.

Bower smiled at that and nodded. "So I assume it's one of my old cases you're working on."

"The Sandy Hunter disappearance."

Pickett was surprised at Bower's reaction. He actually laughed.

"You folks take the hard ones, huh?" Bower asked, shaking his head. "That might be the quickest cold case I ever got. She vanished, but she couldn't. She was there but she shouldn't have been. No family problems, no issues at work. Nice woman, actually happy in life from what we could tell."

"Yet she was there and she did somehow get out of that room," Pickett said. "Got any theories how?"

Bower laughed again. "That kept me awake at nights. I have no flipping idea what happened in there. If I believed in aliens, I would say they beamed her up."

"Room was that clean?" Sarge asked.

"Completely," Bower said. "She walked in that door and

didn't touch a thing. Nothing. I'm not kidding. Aliens or Captain Kirk beamed her into orbit."

They sat there in silence for a moment, then Pickett grabbed her notebook. "I got an idea who we might talk with."

Both Sarge and Bower looked at her.

"We need to talk with a hotel architect," she said, "get the plans for that floor and have an expert go over them."

Bower nodded. "Good idea. We didn't do that."

Sarge was sitting staring just over Bower's head at the wall.

After a moment Bower smiled at Pickett. "Does he do this a lot?"

Before Pickett could answer, Sarge came back into his eyes, then said, "Bower, you said that Hunter was there, but she shouldn't have been. Could that have been someone else?"

"The woman getting out of Hunter's car in the hotel parking garage was wearing the same clothes Hunter had on when leaving home," Bower said. "Same hairstyle, same height, same weight. So it if wasn't her it would have to be a pretty amazingly close double."

"But it would be possible?" Pickett asked.

Bower again laughed. "I think aliens might be possible. Double or not, she didn't walk out of that room."

"And she didn't fly," Sarge said.

"She didn't walk, she didn't fly," Pickett said, "but maybe she crawled. Through a vent or something."

Pickett wished at that moment she had a picture of the look on the two men's faces as they sat there thinking.

Priceless.

CHAPTER SIX

November 16th, 2016
Las Vegas, Nevada

Sarge had enjoyed seeing Bower and some of the others around his old headquarters. But he didn't miss being there at all. They all looked too busy and far too stressed. And he remembered that feeling well.

He didn't miss it.

He liked what he was doing now and he really loved being with Pickett. Her idea of someone crawling out a vent in that hotel was stunning. A long-shot, but stunning.

When they got back to her Grand Cherokee SUV, she didn't even have to start it to turn on the air-conditioning. The slight warmth inside felt good against the chill of the morning air.

She took out her phone and called Robin.

Sarge got out his notebook again so he could write down thoughts and notes they would need.

Pickett put her phone on speaker and Robin answered by asking, "You get anything from Bower?"

"Nothing solid," Pickett said. "But Sarge came up with an idea while talking with him. Can you get the security footage of Hunter leaving her apartment and compare it with the security footage of her going into the hotel?"

Silence for a second on the other end, then Robin said, "Think it might be an imposter?"

"We have the equipment now to find that out," Pickett said, "unlike what they had fourteen years ago."

Sarge nodded to that. It was stunning the advancement in computers in the last fourteen years when it came to facial recognition and everything. And casinos had some of the best technology in the world in those areas to stop known cheaters and criminals.

And it was the casinos that had paid for and updated the police along the way with the same technology. One of the many things not publicized about the casinos helping the city and police.

"I'll get one of Will's experts right on that," Robin said. "Walk patterns, everything, we should know for sure in a couple of hours."

"Great," Pickett said. "Can you access the plans to the hotel area she disappeared in? We're going to go talk with James."

Sarge had no idea who James was, but clearly James and Pickett and Robin were on a first-name basis.

"Think she crawled out, huh?" Robin asked. "I'll dig up the plans."

"I'll call James and see if he is available to meet us, then let you know to send the plans to him."

"Will do," Robin said. "Good ideas."

And she hung up.

Pickett clicked off the phone, then dialed another number. "James," she said. "It's Debra."

"Wonderful," Pickett said after a moment. "Loving the condo. Got an official job-favor to ask of you."

She waited for a second, then smiled at Sarge and said, "Yeah, Cold Poker Gang business."

Sarge was enjoying watching Pickett. One of the many things he really was coming to love about her was how animated she was when she talked. She talked with her hands and head and body movements, even when on the phone. He had no doubt he could just sit and watch her for hours on end.

"Would you take a look at some hotel plans for us?" Pickett asked. "We got a person who vanished out of a hotel room without a trace."

Pickett sat quiet for a moment, her eyes getting bigger and bigger.

"Didn't know that," she said.

Sarge wanted to ask What? What? What? like a little kid, but said nothing.

She nodded a few times. "Thanks, we appreciate it. I'll have Robin send the plans. We'll see you in about twenty minutes."

She clicked off her phone, dialed Robin, said, "Send them." And then hung up again, putting the phone in her pocket.

"Didn't know what?" Sarge asked.

"James said that kids are lost out of locked hotel rooms all the time," she said. "Often never found, sometimes found dead in ducts and plumbing areas and elevator shafts in large hotels. They go in, get lost, and can't get out and no one thinks to look for them inside the walls and ceilings."

Sarge just shook his head. Over the years he had heard about a few cases like that, but always thought it something unusual, not common.

"James said it's almost impossible, however, for a full-sized adult to get into those areas. Accesses are too small for the most part."

Sarge glanced down at his notes. "Sandy Hunter was only just over five feet tall."

Pickett started the car and headed out of the parking lot. For the next minute they both rode in silence.

They might have figured out how Hunter got out of the hotel room. But that was a long, long way from answering why?

And what happened to her?

CHAPTER SEVEN

November 16th, 2016
Las Vegas, Nevada

Pickett really liked James Newell and his wife Patty. Two of the nicer people who had ever lived as far as Pickett was concerned.

James had been the major partner of an international architecture firm based in Las Vegas. He had retired ten years before, but had helped Pickett and Robin on numbers of cases over the years. Pickett and Robin had had many wonderful dinners with him and Patty, as well as the fact that he had helped them solve three cases along the way.

His home was on a seven-acre estate sitting on a rock knoll outside of Vegas, completely protected by a tall decorative fence. The house looked like it fit near the peak of the hill, tucked in and among the huge desert rocks like it had grown there, not been built.

The natural wood and brown tones also helped it fit in. Huge windows looked back out over the valley and the city.

"Wow, this is something," Sarge said as Pickett got them through the gate and headed up the narrow, winding brown-paved road toward the house. The road wound around large rocks and brush like a stream flowing down a narrow canyon.

On the way to the house, she had told Sarge about James and Patty, about how they were good friends, and about how his firm had designed some of the major hotels and buildings around the world.

James greeted them at the large wooden front door with a smile. It had been months since Pickett had seen him and she gave him a big hug before introducing him to Sarge.

James stood tall and distinguished, with a full head of gray hair, long by anyone's standards. His face was full of wrinkles, but mostly from smiling Pickett was sure. The man loved to smile and laugh at most anything.

He had on his normal tan cloth slacks, a tan golf shirt, and tan socks without his normal loafers. Pickett couldn't remember ever seeing him in anything else. Even at major charity events. Patty would dress up, but he would wear the same thing, only adding a tan sweater at times.

When you were that rich and that successful, Pickett figured he could do anything he wanted. He once told her that everyone thought architects were strange, so he just played the part.

"Patty sends her regrets that she missed you," James said as he led them through the fantastic home to an office in the back. The home was made of all natural stone and wood and even though slightly bare, felt welcoming.

Sarge was just sort of staring at things as they walked, his mouth open slightly.

"I just looked at what Robin sent a moment before you got here," James said, indicating that they should watch a white wall. "So we can go over it together."

He clicked a couple keys on a computer terminal and the plans of the hotel came up on a large, blank wall. It was clearly projected on the wall by a projector hidden above it in the ceiling.

It made every room on the hotel plan large and the hallways look huge. Fantastic detail for looking at a plan.

"This is the floor Robin said the woman vanished from in 2002," James said. "Let me highlight the room in green that Robin said she went into."

A moment later one room turned green.

At that moment Pickett's cell rang. It was Robin.

Pickett clicked it on and then put it on speaker and held out the phone. "We're here with James."

"Thanks, James, for helping us on this," Robin said.

"Just getting started," James said. "And Patty sends her best wishes."

"Back at her," Robin said. "And as far as the woman who went into that room you guys are going to study, it was Sandy Hunter. No questions."

Pickett glanced at Sarge who was looking shocked. On the way out to James' house, they had both figured Hunter had been kidnapped before getting to the hotel and switched out.

"One-hundred percent?" Pickett asked.

"One-hundred percent," Robin said. "Bye, James. You guys have fun."

And with that Robin hung up.

"Not what you expected, huh?" James asked.

Pickett just shook her head. "Not at all."

She looked back at the giant floor plan projected on the wall and the green room highlighted on the plan.

What in the world had happened in that room?

And more importantly, why?

CHAPTER EIGHT

November 16th, 2016
Las Vegas, Nevada

Sarge was stunned at the natural beauty of James' home.

The lobby had stone and rough wood and yet it felt warm somehow. And the office he had led them to was huge, the size of two large master bedrooms. Built-in bookshelves covered one wall, another wall was nothing but windows looking out over the valley. A large oak desk occupied one side of the room and some drafting boards and large computers filled another part.

James seemed like a great man, of that there was no doubt. And very willing to help. And Pickett sure seemed fond of him.

"Can we see the heating and cooling plans?" Sarge asked.

James smiled. "I'll lay them over the floor plan."

On the large image on the wall a maze of heating and cooling plans ghosted over the solid floor plan.

"Is that all through the ceiling?" Pickett asked.

"It is," James said, "and no access into it through anything larger than a small vent in the room."

"So heating and cooling is out," Sarge said, feeling disappointed.

"Not really," James said. "This shows all the ducts for delivering the air. Let me clear that off and show you the return-air system. Keeping air moving in a large building is a critical factor. And damned hard to calculate. The newer hotels keep each room or suite as a unit because it's easier to regulate, but the hotels from this time period used central heating and cooling per floor."

The ghost image vanished and then larger ducts appeared, clearly in the walls. It was at that moment that Sarge noticed how thick a few of the walls were.

"Here is what a standard return air vent looks like in that room at that time," James said.

He showed on an area beside the plan a picture of a grated rectangle, clearly just inches from the floor.

"How many of them would be in the room she vanished from?" Pickett asked a moment before Sarge could.

"Two," James said. "Both near the floor. These are the grates children get into and get lost. Hotels do their best to keep them secured tight. Modern return air ducts have moved up near the ceilings, usually over the entrance area and don't ever go outside the room."

Sarge went over to get a better look at the system. The return air duct seemed to dump into a giant square area along with about a quarter of the rooms on the floor. "Does that have duct work in these areas?"

Sarge pointed to the giant square.

"No," James said. "Open air flow. In this hotel there are four of those square room return flow catches. The heating and cooling unit for the floor is there beside it.

"Door into this room I assume," Pickett said.

"There is," James said. "All four of these have a door into the floor's service area."

"Besides getting out onto the same floor," Pickett asked, "are there other ways out of that service room?"

James laughed. "A number. Let me show you."

On the screen the return air ghost image vanished and the floor plan of the large service area in the center of the building came up.

Sarge could see that off that service room were the bank of elevators and also a large square area labeled plumbing."

"So you can get into the elevator service area," Pickett said, "and the plumbing service stack from the large service room on every floor?"

"Yes," James said. "Standard large building design. Especially for the time."

"So exits from every floor from the elevator service area and the plumbing service area?" Sarge asked.

"Yes," James said. "Plus through the roof service area and also all the way to the basement utility room, which is one floor below the parking garage."

"And I assume no security cameras in any of it," Pickett said, shaking her head.

"Likely only at the entrances of each service area, and I wouldn't even count on that in the basement."

Sarge looked around at James. "So a small woman, just over five feet tall, could have undone one of the return air grates and gone inside and put the grate back in place."

"Very easily," James said, nodding. "And with the type of locking screws, she could have screwed the grate back into place from the inside. The grates were designed for workers to move through the passages when needed for cleaning and pest control."

Pickett just laughed.

Sarge shook his head.

"She could have gone in there," Sarge said, "worked her way to the service room, into the elevator shaft and climbed down to the basement and left from there? Possible?"

"Very possible," James said.

Sarge nodded. Now they knew how Sandy Hunter got out of that room, but not any of the whys involved.

Pickett stared at the floor plan, then turned to James. "I know Robin got this plan easily and I'm sure you could have as well, but fourteen years ago, when this hotel was fairly new, who could have gotten the plans?"

James shrugged. "Plans are filed in public. Security areas and cage areas and finance areas are kept a tight secret for each casino, but hotel plans are public."

"So anyone," Pickett said.

"But the key is who would know that this was even possible?" Sarge asked.

James again just shrugged. "Any of the contractors. And on a project this size, there would have been dozens of contractors not counting their employees. And you have to add in any architect or architectural student."

"So Sandy Hunter could have gotten this idea from a thousand different people?" Pickett asked.

James nodded. "At least."

Sarge just sighed and looked back at the floor plan projected on the wall. They had solved the mystery of how Sandy Hunter vanished from the room.

But now they were miles from finding out why she did this and what happened to her.

PART TWO

The Bets Go Up

November 16th, 2016
Las Vegas, Nevada

Pickett called Robin and told her to meet them at the Bellagio Café in twenty minutes for lunch.

"Got some fun stuff for you," Robin said.

Pickett laughed. "We got some stuff to share as well."

Then she got them down the narrow driveway that wound through the rocks and out onto the main road heading back into town. Sarge wasn't saying anything, just sort of staring off into space.

"A real puzzle isn't it?" Pickett asked.

"None of it makes any sense," Sarge said. "And that bothers me a lot. People do things for a reason. Money, love, hate, revenge, and so on. From what the file said about Sandy Hunter, there was no reason for her to do this."

Pickett agreed. Sarge hit on exactly what had been bothering her from the moment Robin said it was actually Sandy Hunter who went into that hotel room.

"So we dig until we find the reason," Pickett said.

Sarge nodded. "I think we take a run at the husband. He might think of something he hadn't thought important when he learns she did it on purpose. And clearly planned it."

"I agree," Pickett said. She wasn't looking forward to that conversation, but she knew Sarge was right, that was the next logical step.

The Bellagio Café had an atmosphere that Pickett flat loved. Brown tones of oak and cloth, with lots of plants between the booths to give each booth a sense of privacy.

The sounds of the casino were like a distant background and even the sound of others talking in the restaurant never seemed to get very loud.

She and Robin had often come here for lunch or dinner when out this far along the Strip. This was her second favorite place and had been happy to learn that it was Sarge's second favorite restaurant as well.

One of the big reasons was that not only was it comfortable, but the food was wonderful and the selection amazing at any time of the day or night.

She had learned from Sarge that Julia and Lott and Andor, the three retired detectives that ran the Cold Poker Gang, also came out here a great deal when on cases. They were nowhere to be seen at the moment.

She and Sarge got seated in a back booth with cloth seats, one of their favorite booths since the first case they met on. It was less than a month ago that she had spent a lot of time in this booth getting to know the handsome man sitting beside her. Now she couldn't imagine not having him beside her.

Amazing how her life had changed in just a short month.

Robin wasn't there yet, so both got coffee and water and menus.

They had both just started to look at the menu when Robin slid into her spot in the booth and put her notebook on the chair.

She had on a light pull-over jacket since the fall air still had a bite to it this morning. It looked police issue, but Pickett knew it wasn't.

"So who gets to go first?" Robin asked, smiling at the two of them.

Sarge laughed. "She seems excited, don't you think?"

Pickett also laughed. "She does. So please go ahead."

Robin smiled and opened her notebook.

"Your idea to check for patterns hit a gold mine," Robin said. "From 1998 until 2015, over ten thousand women have been reported missing and last seen in a hotel in Las Vegas."

"What?" Pickett asked, not even grasping that number.

Robin held up her hand. "Half of those were solved quickly, another quarter of them were run-away women, also solved. No one really missing with any of those. Many others were solved as well one way or another."

"So how many are still cold cases?" Pickett asked.

"About eight hundred," Robin said "over the seventeen years in all the hotels in Vegas. So I sorted for a woman's description matching Sandy Hunter. Size, shape, married, that sort of thing in those eight hundred. And I also took out any disappearance from a newer hotel."

Robin smiled at both of them. Pickett knew that smile. It was clear she had a lot of information and was loving every minute of this.

"So how many?" Sarge asked, shaking his head.

"Eighty-five cases," Robin said. "All similar. A woman who

didn't ever go to a hotel or casino suddenly vanishes into one and is never seen again."

"Eighty-five?" Pickett asked. "That's stunning."

"It gets better," Robin said. "This is a picture of the eighty-five women."

She took out a sheet of paper with eighty-five small thumbnail-sized pictures of women on it. She slid it first to Pickett.

Pickett looked at it. The images were small, all the women looking right into the camera. Clearly driver's license pictures.

All the women had different haircuts and wore different clothing, but something about it seemed odd. She slid the paper to Sarge, who frowned looking at it.

Pickett could feel that something was wrong with the pictures, she just couldn't put her finger on what.

"Here is what I found when I ran the woman's pictures through a facial recognition software," Robin said.

She took out another page and slid it to Pickett.

It had five women on it, all about the same age.

Pickett looked at the smiling face of Robin and then slid the paper to Sarge who sort of snorted.

"All eighty-five missing women are actually only five women?" Pickett asked.

Robin nodded. "All between five foot tall and five-two."

"Any connections at all between them?" Sarge asked.

"All I have is their many married names," Robin said. "Seventeen married or fake names each, actually."

She pointed to the picture of Sandy Hunter. "I'm calling her March because every March she goes missing. Ten times she was married, seven times only engaged. The others each have their own month to vanish."

Pickett sort of sat there stunned. She couldn't even begin to wrap her brain around this.

"Every March?" Sarge asked, his voice soft.

"Every March," Robin said. "She always had different hair color and background and all that. Different job, everything. But no doubt at all it was the same woman every March. The Sandy Hunter case was the only one that actually got her entering a room though. And that was only because Bower took pity on the husband and was ahead of procedure."

Pickett just sat there, stunned.

At that moment the waitress came to take their order, which was a welcome relief to Pickett as she tried to wrap her mind around why a woman would vanish seventeen times in seventeen years.

Five women, actually.

This case just kept getting stranger and stranger.

And bigger and bigger.

CHAPTER TEN

November 16th, 2016
Las Vegas, Nevada

Sarge gave his order to the waitress, but felt like he was almost sleepwalking. Why would the same five women set up a life and then disappear every year? In all his years of being a detective, he had never felt this stunned.

Robin was smiling and Pickett looked as shocked as he felt.

"It took me a good half hour to get past the idea that something like this could happen," Robin said. "And it's something that never would have been caught if we hadn't been trying to dig up leads on this one cold case."

Sarge nodded to that. No chance that any normal investigation would have run a search like Robin did, looking for patterns. Just never would have happened.

"So what's your news?" Robin asked.

Sarge nodded to Pickett that she should go ahead. He wasn't

certain he could even focus on what they had discovered at the moment.

"James showed us how the woman got out of the hotel room," Pickett said. "Because she was so tiny and short, she fit into a return air duct. She went out through the ductwork into a maintenance room, then climbed down an elevator shaft to the sub-basement and went out through the parking garage, more than likely."

"All the security footage from the hotel for three days before and three days after still exist," Robin said. "I'll find out when she got out and now that I know they changed identity, I'll know what to search for."

Sarge nodded, then said what he was sure all of them were thinking. "Why?"

Robin nodded, as did Pickett.

"I have two of Will's best people searching through records of all the left spouses," Robin said. "They had gone through ten of them before I left and not a one reported anything at all missing when their wife vanished. Nothing out of checking, no credit card uses, nothing other than the jewelry and clothes they had on when they vanished."

Again Sarge just shook his head. Not a bit of this was making any sense at all.

"So we have five women," Pickett said, "getting into relationships that last exactly one year before they vanish and change identity."

"They all work regular jobs?" Sarge asked.

"From what we have found so far, yes," Robin said. "Sandy Hunter, our March woman, was pretty typical. Her next time out she worked housekeeping at a second hotel. The year after that she worked at a catering service. I will be working on tracing back their first run at this."

"See if you can find the connection between the five women," Sarge said.

"There has to be one," Pickett said.

At that point the food came and Sarge slowly came to grips with the crazy idea of all this as he ate a French dip sandwich with fries. By the time the waitress took his plate and refilled his coffee, he felt like his mind had returned a little.

"So here is what we know so far on this mess," Sarge said, opening his flip notebook. "First off, we know that the same five women, starting in 1998, vanish from a hotel and each do so on the same month every year."

Robin and Pickett both nodded.

"We are pretty certain that Hunter went out through a return air vent in a hotel room," Sarge said.

Again both women nodded.

Sarge looked at his notes and realized he didn't know one important fact. "Do they always vanish in the same hotel?"

"Three different hotels," Robin said. "They alternate around and all three hotels were built in the same period, so they all would have the same return air systems. But we can check that. I'll have a lot more by dinner. I even have Will fascinated on this case, so he's throwing help at it. Right now he's got two computer specialists digging and has told me he's willing to get more at it if needed."

Sarge nodded. That was great to hear. Not much hid for long from Will and his security people and computer specialists.

Then it dawned on him what he had just thought. "Robin, these women are going to need to create new histories, new ids every year good enough to stand up to some heavy checking for jobs and a driver's license. How would they do that?"

"Shit," Robin said, flipping open her notebook and writing

quickly. "There can't be a lot of people in this city who can do that level of work since 1998. I'll find out."

"So we are still about a thousand miles from the why of all this," Pickett said.

"A sick game to keep five women from becoming bored in life?" Robin asked.

Sarge shrugged. It might be just that, but he had a hunch there was something more going on.

Something much worse.

But he had no idea why he thought that.

CHAPTER ELEVEN

November 16th, 2016
Las Vegas, Nevada

Pickett felt better, more grounded after a BLT sandwich. Over their coffee, they tried to figure out a way to find the motive on all of this. And what the women were even doing.

Robin would go back to her office and try to find out how long it took Sandy Hunter to leave the building after she vanished. And keep chasing any way of finding out how the five women might be connected.

Pickett and Sarge would head to the hotel and see if they could get a tour of the maintenance rooms on the floor Sandy Hunter vanished from. Sarge figured that if they saw the area, it might give them some ideas and Pickett agreed.

Then they all agreed Pickett and Sarge needed to contact and talk to the husband of Sandy Hunter, see if he has anything odd that he remembered. Pickett doubted they would get anything of value, but sometimes it was the smallest detail that broke open a case.

It only took them ten minutes from the Bellagio parking lot to the Bennington parking garage. They went up to the front desk and asked for a manager from security. Sarge flashed his badge and three minutes later a man by the name of Stevenson appeared. He looked to be in his early forties and clearly was management. His hair was balding and he wore a dark suit with a red tie. Pickett could tell he didn't miss a detail, the type of person who worked security in the big hotels.

In fact, she bet Stevenson could read a person across a room and would be dangerous in a poker game.

After introductions, Sarge detailed out what they were doing and wondering if they could see the maintenance area on the 11th floor.

"Can't see why not," Stevenson said. "Always glad to help the police, but if you wanted to see our security areas, I would have needed to get higher permission."

"We can understand that," Pickett said.

Stevenson asked a few quick questions on the elevator ride about the case they were working on. Both Pickett and Sarge said nothing about any other women or regular disappearances. They just gave him the basics of the Sandy Hunter case.

When Stevenson heard the name Sandy Hunter, he laughed. "We get a lot of people who supposedly go missing in the casino, but on that one we still have an open file. You thinking maybe she went out through the return air system?"

"A theory," Pickett said. "That's why we would like to see the maintenance room."

"Only theory I ever had on it as well," Stevenson said, nodding. "But it was before my time here. If you end up solving it, would you let me know so I can close that file?"

"Glad to," Sarge said.

Stevenson waved to the security camera near the maintenance room door, then used a key card to unlock a blank door. It swung open and the lights came up.

The room wasn't that big, about the size of a small bedroom, and was mostly empty. Seven metal doors led off from the room, all closed.

Giant ducts covered the ceiling, all going to the left of the room and vanishing.

Each door was labeled and had no lock on them.

"Heating and cooling there," Stevenson said, pointing to the room where all the large ceiling ducts led. "Elevator there, plumbing stacks there."

He pointed at two doors across from them.

"Mind if we take a look at the elevator shafts?" Sarge asked.

Stevenson nodded and went and opened the door.

Pickett could see the ten elevator shafts. There was a metal ladder on both sides of the huge open area and as they watched from the doorway an elevator flashed upwards.

Below they could see the tops of a few elevators and below them the basement.

"We're thinking she climbed down to the basement and got out that way," Sarge said.

Stevenson nodded. "Doors locked from the outside down there but easy to go out."

"Any security in any of this?" Pickett asked.

"Only on the doors coming into here," Stevenson said.

Stevenson closed the door as another elevator flashed past. Pickett would have been scared to death climbing down that metal ladder, but she had little doubt she could do it if she needed to.

Stevenson went over to the other side of the room and

opened a door. On the other side was a very stark room again the size of a small bedroom. From two sides massive ductwork entered the room just below the ceiling and a massive duct left the room going across the top of the maintenance room.

"They call this a return air cache," Stevenson said. "The air from a quarter of the rooms on this floor flow in here and then goes back to the heating system that pumps air back into the rooms. Even when no heat or air-conditioning is on, the air keeps flowing."

"I thought the return air grates in each room were at floor level," Pickett said, looking up at the massive ducts above them. Ladders built into the walls led up to each one.

"They are," Stevenson said.

"Ladders inside the ducts for maintenance?" Sarge asked.

Carson nodded.

"How often are these ducts cleaned?" Pickett asked.

"April and October," Stevenson said.

"You find things in the ducts?" Sarge asked.

"Oh, sure," Stevenson said, laughing. "Usually money, sometimes dirty movies or sex toys people have stashed behind the grates. One time, a couple years ago, they found a wedding dress. Not at all sure what that was about. By the time the crew gets done with the entire hotel they have a lot I can tell you."

Pickett looked up at the ductwork. "Mind if I climb up and take a look?"

"No trouble," Stevenson said, pulling a tiny flashlight out of his pocket. "You'll need this to see much."

Pickett could tell that Sarge wasn't really pleased with that, but instead of saying anything, he moved to spot her as she climbed quickly up the ladder.

At the top she could sit up easily without bending over, the duct was that large. And she could feel a pretty good breeze blowing on her from the rooms.

She shined her light down the large duct and she could see where there was a hole going down and part of the large main duct turned in both directions.

"It's not all this big beside every room is it?" Pickett asked, looking down at Stevenson and the worried expression on Sarge's face.

"Oh, no," Stevenson said. "On the other side of that it branches and dozens and dozens of narrow ducts drop down to floor level along the hallway. It's an amazing maze."

"Too small for me to get through?" Pickett asked.

"Afraid so, Detective," Stevenson said. "The maintenance people who do those ducts can't be more than five feet tall. They are all women, actually."

"Your staff doesn't do the cleaning?" Sarge asked.

"Nope. But I can give you the company's name that does. They service a number of hotels around town."

Sarge glanced up at Pickett who just smiled. Then she said, "Coming down."

She turned back around and found the ladder rung and went carefully down with Sarge on one side and Stevenson on the other.

About as safe as a person could get on a ladder.

CHAPTER TWELVE

November 16th, 2016
Las Vegas, Nevada

Sarge and Pickett thanked Stevenson for the tour and the name of the cleaning service and headed down to the parking garage for her car. Once in the car, Sarge glanced at Pickett. He held up the name of the service. "You think these folks might have something to do with all this?"

Pickett laughed and took out her phone. "I sure think we should get Robin and Will's people looking into the business, don't you?"

She glanced at it, then said, "No reception."

She handed it to Sarge and got the SUV headed up and out of the parking garage. Once out of the garage, Robin drove for about a block before finding a spot to pull over near a construction site.

She called Robin and told her what they had found. Sarge listened but didn't add anything in. None of this was making sense to him still. Not a bit of it. They were looking at a few puzzle pieces and trying to get a large picture. Wasn't happening.

After Pickett got off the phone with Robin, she got them moving again toward an office at the University of Nevada Las Vegas. Sandy Hunter's husband, Rich, taught there and was more than willing to talk with them about his missing wife.

About eight years ago he had had her declared dead and had gotten remarried. He now had two kids and from what Robin could find, seemed to be doing fine.

Sarge had suggested they not tell him anything about what they had found so far, just explain they were working on the case again because of the Cold Poker Gang.

The university area was full of large trees and shaded. Many of the trees hadn't lost their fall leaves yet so it still seemed lush, something Sarge enjoyed in the spring, summer, and fall. But today the shade made everything feel colder.

Professor Hunter's office was in an older brick building that had the feeling of an old library. His office was on the second floor and the wooden staircase in the building was wide and the wood smoothed almost white in the center of the stairs by so much traffic.

They knocked on the old wooden office door and a bald man with a wide smile greeted them, inviting them in and offering them chairs in front of his desk. Sarge wondered how many students over the last decade had sat in exactly those chairs.

Hunter was clearly a smart man who seemed, at least outwardly, happy. Kind of sad that a nice guy like him had been taken by whatever scam the five women were pulling.

"So you are looking into Sandy's disappearance after all

these years," Hunter said as he sat down. "Can I ask why, detectives?"

Pickett explained how they were basically retired and on a special task force trying to solve old cold cases. Sandy's case had just come up.

"Not at all sure what I can add," Hunter said, "that I didn't already tell Detective Bower and his partner."

"We just want to look at everything again," Sarge said. "Sometimes time can bring up all sorts of things that seemed normal but through the perspective of time now seem odd. Anything like that?"

Hunter seemed to think for a moment, slowly shaking his head.

"When did you first meet Sandy?" Pickett asked.

Hunter shrugged. "About two years before she disappeared."

Sarge sat back, stunned at that.

Picket glanced at Sarge, then followed up her question before Hunter could tell anything seemed odd. "Were you dating that first year?"

"Oh, heavens, no," Hunter said. "I would just run into her on campus, usually about once or twice a month and we would talk. She didn't give me her address and phone number until about a year before she vanished and we were married eight months later."

Sarge slowly let out the breath he had been holding. These women found and set up their next relationships before vanishing from the previous one. Amazing.

Simply amazing.

And very damned cold-blooded.

"So did you ever meet any of Sandy's family?"

"All dead," Hunter said. "Back when she was a kid. She was raised in the system back east in Boston."

"She have friends?" Pickett asked.

"A few close friends from college and a few at work," Hunter said. "Everyone liked her. I loved her."

Sarge leaned forward slightly. "You ever meet the friends from college?"

Hunter shook his head. "They were scattered around the country, so never did even though she said she wanted me to meet them. I e-mailed them to let them know she was missing. Got a few e-mails back, but I kind of had the feeling they blamed me."

Pickett glanced at Sarge. He had a hunch they were both thinking the same thing, that her friends from college were the other four women.

"And you had no indication anything was wrong the day she vanished, or the weeks leading up to it?" Sarge asked.

"Nothing at all," Hunter said. "Everything was exactly as it had been those three months of marriage. She seemed happy, actually."

"And nothing vanished with her?" Pickett asked.

Hunter shook his head. "Just her clothes and her engagement and wedding ring is all, and whatever else she had in her purse. She seldom carried much money, liked to use her debit card for things."

"We talked with Detective Bower," Sarge said, "who said that her cards were never used. That right?"

Hunter nodded. "She vanished without a trace."

"You ever think you see her again around town?" Pickett asked.

Hunter laughed. "Oh, sure, for the first year or so I thought I saw her everywhere. But I was wrong every time. A counselor told me that was normal for people in my position."

Sarge didn't want to tell him that he might have been right a few of those times.

"So was she ever gone in the year you knew her?" Pickett asked.

Hunter sat back for a moment, clearly thinking back over time. "Yeah, she went to visit two of her college friends for five days a month after we met. Then in the fall she took another trip up to Seattle, I think she said to stay with another friend there for five days, a month before our wedding. Said she was trying to convince her friend to come down and stand up for her in the wedding."

"She didn't, I assume," Pickett asked.

"Gloria, a friend from work, did the honors," Pickett said. "Might want to talk with Gloria if you can find her. She and Sandy seemed to have gotten very close. She might know more than I do."

They thanked Professor Hunter after a couple more questions and headed back out to Pickett's car without talking.

When Pickett closed her door, Sarge turned to her and asked, "Where do you think Sandy went on those two vacations?"

Pickett shrugged. "Not a clue. But I wouldn't bet against the timing being the same timing as that cleaning company cleaning out the vents in those two hotels."

Sarge just looked at her, surprised. "Why?"

Pickett shrugged as she got the car started. "No idea why. Not a damn bit of this is making any sense."

"Now that I agree with," Sarge said.

CHAPTER THIRTEEN

November 16th, 2016
Las Vegas, Nevada

Pickett called Robin from the car and she didn't have much yet, but would meet them for dinner at the buffet at Golden Nugget. The only time the three of them went there was while they were on a case. It felt almost like an office to them.

Sarge and Pickett spent the next hour talking with Gloria, Sandy's friend. Gloria had not aged well which had to do with the almost two hundred pounds she had gained since she knew Sandy.

And Gloria knew even less than Rich had known about Sandy.

So Pickett took them back to the Ogden and parked in her spot, then they walked down Fremont Street to the Golden Nugget. It was still a nice evening, but they both took jackets because they knew the walk back would be chilly.

Pickett felt frustrated by this entire thing. They had made a lot of progress in one day, going from a woman vanishing into a hotel room to understanding how she got out and that five women were doing this regularly.

But they had no idea why, or how to find the woman that for one year called herself Sandy.

The smell of pizza and prime rib in the buffet made Pickett realize just how hungry she was. It had only been four hours since lunch, but a draining four hours talking with the husband and old friend.

Robin wasn't there yet, so Sarge paid for all three of them since it was his turn. Since all three of them didn't have any issue with money, they had decided a few weeks back to just alternate paying for dinners and lunches. Just easier that way.

Then he and Pickett left their jackets at their normal table and went to get food.

Ten minutes later Robin joined them and within fifteen minutes they were all eating.

Pickett had gone for some prime rib, some breaded shrimp, and a pretty large salad with eggs. Sarge had his normal prime rib, ham, and potatoes. Robin always started with just a salad, fairly plain.

"So," Sarge said after a few minutes to Robin, "Any luck on trying to find out a connection between the five women?"

"Nothing yet," Robin said, shaking her head. "We are pretty convinced that this started for all of them in 1998. And that they were all in their early twenties. But their original identities seem to be very, very well hidden."

"So five women," Pickett said, "suddenly decide to become other women, marry or get into relationships, and then just vanish every year?"

"Pretty much," Robin said, finishing her salad and standing and heading for her main course.

"So back there in 1998 we have five women who knew each other," Sarge said, shaking his head as he cut at his prime rib, "suddenly vanish from their lives and start new lives, strings of new lives."

"Think we need to look for some event that had five friends involved?" Pickett asked. "Something that would have triggered whatever they are doing now."

"It would sure help if we could figure out why they were pulling the vanishing act every year," Sarge said.

Robin came back as they sat there eating and thinking. Around them the noise of the buffet felt like a welcoming background sound. There was just something about people laughing and enjoying themselves that made an atmosphere comfortable.

"I do have some news about the cleaning service," Robin said as she worked to put some sour cream on a baked potato. "There is no connection at all to any of the women and the company cleans all the time and has upwards of fifty hotels as clients. All their cleaners are from twenty to twenty-five. None older."

"Dead end," Sarge said.

"Completely," Robin said.

Pickett shook her head. "I would have lost that bet. I thought there was a chance the months of disappearances of the women matched the months of the cleaning for some reason."

Robin shook her head. "Nope. No connection anywhere. None of them ever worked for the company either."

Pickett felt disappointed in that. For some reason she was convinced the disappearances had to do with those return air ducts. No idea why she thought that, but she did.

"Any pattern to the months the five women disappear?" Sarge asked.

"Every other month for ten months," Robin said, "January,

March, May, July, September. Same woman uses the same month every year."

"So we are past the last one," Pickett said.

Robin nodded. "Missing person's case on the last September one is still active but cold. As all eighty-five of the cases with these five women are."

"These five women's disappearing acts have sure been brutal to a lot of good people," Sarge said.

Pickett could tell he was really disgusted. She felt the same way.

CHAPTER FOURTEEN

November 16th, 2016
Las Vegas, Nevada

It wasn't until Sarge was working on a wonderful cheesecake that he remembered to ask if Robin had discovered when Sandy left the hotel.

"She didn't," Robin said. "I have one of Will's people going over facial recognition of all the security footage in the file one more time, but for three days after she vanished into that hotel, she did not leave. We're pretty sure of that."

Pickett had been sipping on a glass of wine and she looked startled. As startled as Sarge felt.

"She sure didn't stay in those return air ducts," Pickett said.

Sarge knew instantly what had happened. "Robin, is it still possible to get the room reservations from that hotel for that time?"

"Sure," Robin said, nodding. "You thinking she had a room for a few days?"

"Starting the day before," Pickett said. "I've been wondering how she would have gotten a change of clothes, new hair color, and so on. If she had a room booked the day before, she could have had clothes already there."

"And she would have been able to get into it easily through the return air system," Sarge said nodding.

Robin had out her notebook and was taking notes. "I'm thinking she would have stayed a full week. But this is going to be hard to narrow down."

"The names would be fake, more than likely a couple's name," Pickett said.

Sarge agreed. That was exactly what he was thinking.

"And if we can find that fake name, it might lead us to their next name," Robin said.

Both Sarge and Pickett shook their heads at that.

"I wouldn't expect that," Sarge said. "All signs are that these women are very, very careful and have been for a lot of years."

"Can't hurt to check, though," Pickett said.

"Agreed," Robin said. "So we have a pretty good idea how each woman vanishes now. But not one idea as to why."

"Or even who they are," Pickett said.

With that, they all sat in silence and then went back to working on their desserts.

Thirty minutes later Robin headed for home.

Sarge took Pickett's hand once they got out of the hotel and they headed up Fremont toward the Ogden condos. The air had a solid bite to it as he had expected and he was glad he had grabbed a jacket.

"Beautiful night," Pickett said as the strolled along once they got past the party atmosphere of the Fremont Street Experience.

Sarge had to agree. Even with the cold chill, the night was peaceful and the air clear and fresh.

"You up for a movie?" he asked after a half block. "Get our minds off of this crazy case."

"I'd love that," Pickett said, squeezing his hand.

When they reached the top floor of the Ogden, Pickett opened her door and he opened his, leaving it slightly open for her to follow in a few minutes. She needed to feed Nose her nightly treat and change her clothes. Pickett usually wore sweatpants and a sweatshirt around her condo and had started doing that when she came over.

Basically, he did the same.

He first gave Pete and Ree a snack and when they were munching away, he got out the popcorn machine and got it ready, then he went to change clothes. By the time he finished, Pickett and Nose were in the kitchen and she was picking up the cat dishes, rinsing them off, and putting them in the dishwasher.

The three kittens were already scampering off to play down the hallway toward the bedroom. He couldn't imagine living in this place without those kittens, now.

And living here without Pickett at his side.

As far as he was concerned, two retired detectives and three cats made a perfect family.

As the popcorn was starting, Pickett said, "Got a phone call from my friend Jean on my machine."

Sarge nodded. Pickett still had a home phone and all her friends had been trained to call her there for personal stuff.

"Jean said the secretary my ex left with has now left him."

Pickett was smiling and shaking her head.

Pickett's husband, about five years before, had left with his twenty-something secretary. That was why Pickett had enough money to buy the wonderful condo next door. Her settlement had been enough to buy the condo and have enough to live the rest of her life without even getting her retirement payments from the city.

Sarge and his former wife had parted on good terms about seven years before. Being a detective had basically killed that marriage, Sarge had no doubt.

"Think he's going to contact you?" Sarge asked.

Pickett just laughed. "Not a chance in hell. He always hated it when I was right and I got a hunch he's remembering my last words to him."

"And what were they?" Sarge asked, smiling.

"Nothing nasty," Pickett said. "I just told him to get as much as he could as often as he could from the young thing because it wasn't going to last."

Sarge laughed and Pickett just grinned.

"Karma is a bitch, isn't it?" Pickett said.

Sarge could only agree as three kittens streaked past the kitchen area, making enough noise to pretend to be a herd of elephants. Amazing that three creatures so small could make so much noise.

They even drowned out the popping corn.

PART THREE

Mucking the Hand

CHAPTER FIFTEEN

November 17th, 2016
Las Vegas, Nevada

Pickett finished her omelet and sat back sipping on her morning coffee in the Golden Nugget Buffet. The normal customers and tourists were mostly on the other side of the restaurant, near the windows looking out over the pool area. The morning walk to breakfast had been chilly, but invigorating.

And the movie last night had been wonderful. They had decided to watch the original Ghostbusters movie, since when it first came out they had both been too busy with work to see it. It was wonderfully silly and just what she had needed.

And curling up next to Sarge and falling asleep with three kittens sleeping in different places around the bedroom had also been perfect as well. She wasn't sure how she had gotten so lucky to have him enter her life, but she was going to enjoy it as long as it lasted.

And he said he felt the same way.

Robin had met them for breakfast with a ton of reports she had generated last night, more than likely working while they were enjoying watching a giant marshmallow man roam the streets of New York.

Each report was the missing person's case on the women. All eighty-five times someone had cared enough to file a missing person's report. These five women had hurt a lot of people along the way with whatever they were doing.

Robin had then called each woman by the name of the month she vanished every year and done a summary of the jobs, traits, hair colors, looks, and so on for all five.

After Sarge finished looking at the last summary, Pickett asked, "Patterns at all that we could use to pinpoint who they are at the moment?"

"Nothing," Robin said. "All the changes seem to be random. Even the types of car they drive changes from incarnation to incarnation."

"They are all in their late thirties, now," Sarge said, "How are they aging?"

Robin dug through a file and pulled out pictures of all five from the last disappearance cycle. Pickett studied them. There was nothing at all outstanding about them. Attractive late-thirties women. Nothing more.

"The detectives on the last cycle of disappearances got DNA samples of the women from the last husbands and boyfriends and have them in the system," Robin said. "No hits at all as to history. But they are sisters."

"Sisters?" Pickett asked, shocked. She couldn't believe that all five were sisters.

Robin nodded. "Sisters. We are running DNA searches for any close or other family match in the system around the country, but that's going to take days. If not longer."

"But next time they vanish and the DNA is collected, it will hit," Sarge said.

Pickett nodded. "I'm betting they know that and don't care."

"Certainly won't help us find them now," Robin said.

"And the very first disappearances were as fake as all the others?" Sarge asked.

"They were," Robin said. "As best as we can find, all five sisters appeared out of the blue and got fake names and started into a new life."

"But why?" Sarge asked.

Robin only shrugged.

Pickett sipped on her coffee and Sarge leafed through the files as Robin went to get something more to eat.

The five women, five sisters, had to be doing this for a reason. And a carefully planned reason right from the start.

They weren't taking anything, they weren't actually hurting anyone in a criminal way. Pickett knew there wasn't a law saying it was against the law to run away from a life. So on the surface these women were doing nothing against the law.

On the surface.

But why would five sisters start down this road? None of this made any sense at all.

Pickett looked around at all the tourists enjoying their morning in the buffet. Maybe the view on this case was too narrow. People came into Las Vegas from all over the world. These five women had to have been from somewhere.

Robin put a plate of French toast in front of her chair and grabbed her napkin and sat down. As she bit into the toast, Pickett asked, "Where are these women from?"

"No idea," Robin said.

Sarge was looking at Pickett with his puzzled expression, so she went on.

"Is there a way to find out if say five sisters vanished somewhere in 1997 or 1998 at the same time?" Pickett asked. "All short, young women. Wouldn't that be in a file somewhere?"

Robin nodded, wiping off her hands and taking her pen and making a note. "Sure worth a computer search."

Sarge nodded, then suddenly grabbed the picture of Sandy Hunter at thirty-nine. "Computer search gave me an idea. You think these mid-to-late-thirties women might use a dating service to find the next husband?"

Pickett laughed and Robin again wiped off her hands from the syrup from her waffle and took notes.

"It will take some time to run facial recognition on the major dating sites around the time the women disappeared," Robin said. "But again, worth the search."

Pickett shook her head. "I doubt you will find anything. These women line up their next husbands a year ahead of leaving the last one."

"That's right," Sarge said.

"Still worth a search," Robin said.

"So you got some things to do," Pickett said to Robin. "Got any ideas about what we could do?"

"Ex-husbands," Robin said, sliding two folders toward Pickett. "Here is everything about March's last two husbands. Both of them are technically still married to her. Maybe one of them has something to add to this craziness."

"You thinking that after seventeen times," Sarge said, "Sandy Hunter, aka March, might be getting sloppy."

"One can only hope," Robin said.

Pickett could only agree to that statement. She had no doubt it was going to take some luck and more than likely a mistake one of the women made to break this open. And so far these five sisters didn't seem to be the types to make mistakes.

CHAPTER SIXTEEN

November 17th, 2016
Las Vegas, Nevada

Robin left and Sarge and Pickett sat and worked on their coffees while reviewing the files of the last two times Sandy Hunter had vanished. Two years ago her name had been Karen Dross and last year she had been named Kathy Charles.

They decided that they should talk to her husband Buddy Charles first, so Sarge got on the phone to the Detective Guy from the University Station who had caught the case. It was still an active case, so they needed to get the detective in charge permission to talk with Buddy Charles.

Detective Guy just laughed. "Be my guest. That case was cold from the first moment it hit my desk."

"Yeah, kind of like the one we're working," Sarge said. "Not sure if there's a connection, but we'll let you know if there is. Anything you can tell us about this Buddy Charles?"

"Nice guy, but really torn up that his new wife suddenly vanished. He's blaming himself even though he had absolutely nothing to do with it. Calling me every week for an update I just don't have."

"We'll see if we can talk him off the ledge a little," Sarge said. "Maybe give him some faith that the police are working on it."

"Thanks," Detective Guy said. "I think anything's going to help the guy."

Sarge hung up and looked at Pickett who had been listening.

"Put on your counselor hat," Sarge said. "We got a husband taking this really hard. And can't say as I blame him."

"Neither can I," Pickett said. "I wonder how many of the husbands didn't make it through this?"

Sarge just sort of shuddered and stood. "Not a question I want Robin looking into."

"Yeah, with that I agree."

It took them fifteen minutes to walk back to the Ogden as they had been doing every morning now for a month. Sarge loved the routine and the blocks of exercise. It wasn't much, but the walk to the casino and back every day made him feel like he was doing a little something.

Most days since he had met Pickett they had managed to spend a little time in the condo's exercise room. But he honestly liked walking more, especially walking with Pickett.

Pickett again drove. She liked to drive and it didn't stress her out and he didn't mind her driving in the slightest. In fact, he was pretty convinced she was a better driver than he was. So after just weeks of working together, they were already in a habit of her driving.

Pickett had called Buddy Charles at his work and asked if

they could talk and he was more than welcoming. He was the CEO of a major grocery chain and they met him in his main store in his office suite. There was no doubt at all to Sarge that this guy had money.

He looked to be about forty, with a slight paunch and graying hair combed back. He stood about Sarge's height and seemed in shape. He had his suit jacket draped over the back of his desk chair and his tie loosened. The office was on the second floor and looked out at the Strip. A picture of his wife, Kathy, still occupied the corner of his desk.

Sarge and Pickett both identified themselves and showed their badges, then took seats in front of his large oak desk.

"So why more detectives on Kathy's disappearance?" Buddy said as they sat down. "Did something come up?"

"We're working all sorts of paths on this," Pickett said. "Detective Guy will call you at once if we have any leads?"

Buddy nodded and Sarge could see instantly what Detective Guy was talking about. This man was really, really depressed.

"We need to ask some personal questions about Kathy if you don't mind," Sarge said.

"Not at all," Buddy said. "Anything you think might help."

"When and how did you two meet?" Sarge asked.

"About two years ago now," Buddy said. "My first wife and I had divorced about five years ago and I was eating lunch at a little diner around the corner from here and she came in. We got talking and ended up running into each other a few other times until I finally got up the nerve to ask her out in April. We were married four months later."

Sarge nodded and wrote all that down in his notebook. It fit the pattern of the women setting up the men while still with the previous husband.

"So before she vanished, did you sense anything was wrong?" Pickett asked.

"Nothing," Buddy said, shaking his head. "I thought we were happy. She sure seemed happy."

"Did she have any old friends?" Sarge asked. "Friends she traveled with?"

"Yeah," Buddy said. "Some old girlfriends back east. She got together with them twice while we were together."

"Did she say where?"

"She said she was going to Seattle in April, but turned out she went to San Francisco."

Sarge glanced at Pickett who suddenly sat forward.

"How did you know that?" Pickett asked.

"I had only known this woman for a month," Buddy said. "I got a lot of money and I would rather have that money go to my kids from my first wife than someone trying to take me. So I had her followed."

Sarge nodded. "Very smart. Did she meet some old friends?"

"She did," Buddy said. "Four other women around her age. They spent most of the time in a big suite in an older hotel there. Then she came home."

"She tell you about the change in plans?" Pickett asked.

"She did," Buddy said. "And I didn't even ask."

Sarge glanced at Pickett. The women knew they were being followed. And if Sarge was to bet, the hotel had return air ducts they could go in and out of in disguise.

But at least now they knew the five sisters got together for some reason twice a year. Still no idea why, but at least that was a start.

"Did you hire a professional to follow her?" Pickett asked.

Buddy nodded. "Sure did."

"You still have the report?"

Buddy shrugged and stood and went to a file cabinet built into one wall. He unlocked it and pulled out the report and handed it to Pickett. "You can keep it. Not doing me much good now at all."

"You hire a firm to try to find her?" Sarge asked.

Again Buddy nodded. "No damn luck. Last she was seen was going into the Benning Casino and Hotel. One of the other women from her job was supposed to meet her there in the café for lunch, but Kathy never showed in the restaurant. Just vanished into thin air. Her car was still in the basement parking garage."

Sarge knew exactly how she had vanished. She had found a camera dead area, put on a wig and a change of clothes, and then went into a guest room that was already reserved. But he didn't tell Buddy that. They just didn't dare yet.

"She took nothing?" Pickett asked.

"Her clothes she was wearing and the jewelry she had on. I had bought her a wonderful gold and diamond necklace and it was still in her jewelry box. She didn't take anything from me except my love and my pride."

"It isn't your fault, you know," Pickett said. "Things happen to good people."

"I know that here," Buddy said, pointing to his head. "But my gut and my heart tells me otherwise."

"Was it a happy year with her?" Sarge asked.

Buddy nodded.

"Then treasure that for the moment until we find out what happened. Sometimes a good year is a lot more than many couples get."

Buddy nodded and looked at the picture of Kathy on his desk. "I know that."

"You need to believe it," Pickett said.

"And that I'm still trying to do," Buddy said, staring at the picture.

All Sarge could do was sit there and be angry. Why in the world were these five sisters destroying so many men's lives?

They took nothing, but at the same time they took everything.

CHAPTER SEVENTEEN

November 17th, 2016
Las Vegas, Nevada

Pickett and Sarge walked out to her SUV in silence after leaving Buddy's office. Pickett just felt angry and she could tell that Sarge was as upset as she was.

She got into the car and they both just sat there in silence, letting the muffled traffic noise filter in. The day was starting to warm up a little, but not enough that she needed to turn on the air-conditioning. The sun actually felt good.

"On second thought," Sarge said, breaking the silence, "I think we need to get Robin and Will and their computers on finding out exactly what happened to these eighty-five men these women have destroyed."

"You think they are doing this on purpose?" Pickett asked, staring at the man she was quickly coming to love more than she wanted to admit.

"They are clearly doing this on purpose," Sarge said. "But if it's just for cover for something else, I don't know. But I do know they are heartless."

"With that I agree," Pickett said, taking out her cell phone and calling Robin. She quickly detailed out what they were looking for, then hung up.

"So let's take a look at the private-eye report," Sarge said.

Pickett opened the folder and leaned toward him, letting him see the basic contents. The first thing in the folder was a picture of the woman they were calling March, formally Sandy Hunter and four other women. This picture was labeled Kathy Charles. She was aging well from the pictures they had of her in the Sandy Hunter file. One of those women who didn't show many wrinkles and someone who had kept good care of herself.

The next picture was of the five sisters, all sitting around a restaurant table, eating. From the picture they seemed to be happy and enjoying themselves.

Pickett had no doubt it was the five women who kept vanishing every year.

"What happened that would cause these five sisters to dedicate seventeen years of their lives to meeting and leaving husbands?" Sarge asked, staring at the picture.

Pickett could only shake her head. Nothing at all made sense. Nothing. But something must have set the women on this course. Pickett and Sarge just needed to find out who the women had been originally and search their pasts, their real pasts for the clues.

They spent the next thirty minutes sitting in the car reading the private detective's report. Nothing at all new or unusual.

Pickett closed the file, then looked at Sarge. "Think this guy might give us some information not in the report?"

She pointed to the name on the report.

Sarge nodded. "He's the only one who has seen the five·

sisters together recently. Let's check him out with Robin and then ask Buddy to call the guy and tell him it would be all right to talk with us."

Pickett nodded. She agreed. There might be something.

She took out her phone and called Robin and put the phone on speaker.

"Anything?" Robin asked without saying hello.

"Not much from Charles," Pickett said, "but he had a private detective follow his soon-to-be wife on her meeting with her sisters."

"Did you get the report?" Robin asked, suddenly sounding excited. "And who was the agency?"

"Strickland Investigations," Pickett said. "H. Strickland was the guy who filed the report. Nothing in the report we didn't know."

"The guy is reputable," Robin said. "Will does work with him at times."

"We think it might not hurt to go talk with him," Pickett said. "See what is not in the report to the client. Would you set it up with him since Will knows him and we'll get permission from Buddy Charles to have him talk with us."

"Got it," Robin said. "And on the question about the husbands you asked earlier. All but two of them are still alive. One died of cancer, the other in a skiing accident. They all seemed to recover given time from their year with one of the sisters."

"Good," Sarge said, nodding.

Pickett felt relieved.

"I'll call you right back," Robin said, "as soon as I get in touch with Strickland."

Robin hung up and quickly dialed Buddy Charles.

Three minutes later they had Charles' permission to talk

with his investigator and Strickland would be waiting for them in his office.

A very busy morning so far. Pickett liked that. She just wished they were making progress toward the reason behind all this.

But as Sarge said as she started up the car to head for Strickland's office. "At least we have solved eighty-five missing persons' cold cases."

Normally, that would be really something. But something else was going on here besides five sisters unable to stay in relationships. She could just feel it.

CHAPTER EIGHTEEN

November 17th, 2016
Las Vegas, Nevada

Sarge had an odd feeling about Henry Strickland from the moment they shook hands. Henry was a short man, not more than five-four, if that. He looked like any tourist visiting Las Vegas from the Midwest. His slightly graying hair was combed back, his loud Hawaiian shirt had more colors than the Vegas Strip, and he wore Bermuda shorts and white socks and black dress shoes.

Perfect Las Vegas tourist, even in November. Sarge would have walked past him without a second look.

Strickland's outer office was a sprawling modern complex with a dozen young people working computers, all dressed very casually. His office had a massive mahogany desk, windows that looked out over a golf course, and a bathroom off to one side that looked as modern as one of Sarge's bathrooms in his penthouse condo.

Clearly there was money in private investigation. Of course, Sarge knew that since Robin's husband Will was one of the richest people he had ever met and he did security and investigation as well.

Strickland pointed to two chairs in front of his desk and went around behind the desk to drop into a large, leather chair.

Pickett glanced back out the office window at all the people at the desks. "Can I ask what all those people are doing?"

"Background searches, mostly," Strickland said. "We hire out to churches, casinos, you name it, to do background searches on possible new employees."

Sarge nodded. That made complete sense. Someone had to do that sort of thing.

"So I got this call from Buddy Charles," Strickland said, leaning forward, "saying you two are looking into his wife's disappearance."

"His and others," Sarge said. "And he let us have your report about her trip to San Francisco, but we were wondering if there was more you didn't put in the report."

Strickland shrugged and opened a file in front of him on his desk. "I got this out when I heard you were coming and looked at it again. This is a duplicate of the file I gave Charles."

Sarge and Pickett both watched as Strickland looked quickly at the report, then nodded and closed it. "Only thing I didn't tell Buddy was that I was sure the five women knew that I was following them."

"We kind of figured as much," Pickett said. "When she told him about the new location."

Strickland nodded.

Sarge watched Strickland and he didn't seem at all surprised by that news.

"Let me tell you something else odd," Strickland said. "They spent most of their time in one suite. All of them had their own rooms, under varied names, but they also had a large suite that was separate. After they all headed to the airport I bribed a nice hotel maid to tell me what she had seen in that room. She said she had seen computers. Five computers set up around the suite."

Sarge sat back, surprised.

"Seriously?" Pickett asked.

"Big new Mac laptops," Strickland said, nodding. "The maid said she was hoping to save for one for her grandchild. I gave her a few hundred to help in the cause for her information."

"What would five sisters be doing with the laptops?" Pickett asked.

"Sisters?" Strickland asked, learning forward.

"Sisters," Sarge said.

He and Pickett and Robin had agreed on the way to see Strickland that he could be trusted and it wouldn't hurt to get his take on all of this. Since no crime had been committed that they knew about, letting Strickland into the investigation wouldn't hurt anything.

And besides, they figured they needed all the help they could get.

"Let me get you some more information," Pickett said, taking out her phone. "Robin and Will say you can be trusted, so we thought we would bring you completely into this to see if you have any ideas on just what in the world is going on."

"This is sounding stranger and stranger," Strickland said, smiling.

Sarge laughed. "You have no idea."

"Robin, please e-mail Mr. Strickland the photos we talked about and the page of details for each woman."

Pickett nodded, said thanks, and hung up.

Strickland had already turned and was bringing online his large desktop computer that sat to one side of his desk.

Sarge sat there, watching the investigator as he opened his e-mail and clicked on what Robin had sent him.

"Okay," Strickland said. "I'm seeing a picture of a lot of women. What is that all about?"

"Eighty-five of them," Sarge said. "All gone missing without a trace over the last seventeen years. Click on the next picture."

Strickland did and then sat back. "Are you telling me the same five women were those other eighty-five women?"

"They are all the same," Pickett said. "And we know from DNA from their last two disappearances that the five are all sisters."

"They meet a guy," Sarge said, "usually marry him, and then vanish without a trace, taking nothing but their clothes. No robbery, no reason, nothing."

"Exactly like Charles' wife did," Strickland said.

Sarge nodded. "That's why when we discovered you had actually seen all five together, we needed to bring you into this investigation."

Strickland nodded. "No idea who they are originally, I assume."

"Not yet," Pickett said. "We have an international search for anything family related on DNA. That's our best hope there."

"And no idea who they are with and what their names are now?"

"No idea," Sarge said. "Or if they are even continuing on. We are betting they are."

Strickland nodded. "I've trailed my fair share of women getting together for a few days of fun and friendship. These five felt different. They played all the parts, but they didn't seem to be really having fun. Just a gut thing."

"So this was some sort of planning meeting," Pickett said.

Sarge agreed. "And they meet like this twice a year."

"We need to figure out why and what they were doing on those computers," Strickland said.

Sarge just laughed. "That would sure help."

Strickland smiled. "I know a guy who just might be able to help us."

"Help us with what?" Pickett asked.

"Find out what those women were doing on those computers in that hotel," Strickland said.

"That was a year-and-a-half ago," Sarge said. "How would that be possible?"

Suddenly Pickett started laughing. She patted Sarge's arm. "He's talking about Mike Dans."

"Oh," Sarge said, shaking his head.

Strickland just smiled and said nothing, but it was clear Pickett was right. They were about to call the best computer expert in Las Vegas, the one who did things reputable agencies like Strickland's and Robin's husband couldn't do.

CHAPTER NINETEEN

November 17th, 2016
Las Vegas, Nevada

Pickett really liked and respected Mike Dans, even though she knew sometimes his methods didn't follow the strict letter of the law.

Mike and his girlfriend, Heather Voight, often worked with Julia and Lott and Andor on Cold Poker Gang cases. And Mike really enjoyed helping out the Cold Poker Gang as much as possible.

Sarge said he had met Mike on a robbery case about ten years before and liked him. Mike was a former Special Forces guy who hadn't lost a step or a bit of muscle. He kept his hair short and had an infectious smile that hid a brilliant mind.

He also controlled a small army of Special Forces retired soldiers for all sorts of jobs, many off the books. It was that group of highly-trained men that had rescued hundreds of prisoners from tunnels under Las Vegas just a month ago. Mike and his people took no credit or payment. They had just done what they had needed to do.

Mike had done Sarge favors at times over the years and Pickett knew that Sarge had done a few in return. Mike ran a security firm, only not a famous one like Robin's husband's firm, but a firm that stayed behind the scenes.

Mike and his people were also experts in all sorts of computer issues. And Mike was the best of them all.

Pickett knew that Mike's firm worked for Will at times, and it didn't surprise her that he also worked for Strickland's firm when needed.

They decided that Sarge should call Mike, since that would help Strickland keep his hands clean a little more. So as Sarge dialed Mike's number, Strickland excused himself to use the restroom.

From Sarge's side of the conversation that Pickett could hear, Mike seemed happy to hear from them. They hadn't talked with Mike since the amazing work that he and his team did a month ago.

"So," Sarge said after a few moments of talking with Mike, "we have found ourselves in another strange case."

Sarge laughed and nodded. "Yeah, seems we attract them. Right now I am sitting in Henry Strickland's office with Pickett. Henry has excused himself to go use the restroom while I talk with you. The reason I am calling is that we could sure use some help."

Pickett watched as Sarge nodded. "Here is what we need. In April of 2015, five women stayed in a high-end hotel in San Francisco. They each had their own room, but they also rented a suite where they worked for three days on computers. Any chance we could figure out anything about what they were doing?"

Sarge nodded, then said, "Worth a try. At this point anything will help. I'll have Strickland send you the entire file, since he did surveillance on the five women."

"Thanks, Mike," Sarge said. "Make sure you charge me for your time on this. Full rate."

Sarge laughed and then hung up.

Pickett smiled. "I'm betting he said his full rate was lunch, right?"

"Right," Sarge said.

At that moment Strickland came out of the bathroom. "I keep telling him he works too cheap."

Strickland sat down at his computer and two minutes later turned away. "Mike's got the entire report. Now, explain to me how you got started on all this."

Pickett laughed and for the next fifteen minutes they filled Strickland in completely on the cold case of Sandy Hunter that opened this can of worms and how she got out of the hotel room and so on.

All Strickland did was sit, looking stunned, with his mouth open slightly.

Pickett knew that feeling. This case tended to do that to people.

PART FOUR

Drawing a Dead Hand

CHAPTER TWENTY

November 17th, 2016
Las Vegas, Nevada

Sarge sipped at the iced tea the waitress at the Bellagio Café had brought him. It tasted great after a morning of interviews and no real progress. Strickland had helped some in making this a focus and had got the information to Mike Dans that Mike would need to have any hope of doing any tracing.

On the way to lunch from Strickland's office, Pickett had explained to Sarge how it might be possible for Mike to find out some information about what those women were doing, even a year-and-a-half later. It was going to depend on how the hotel internet connections worked and if they stored usage data on the cloud.

Sarge took away from what Pickett said that what Mike was doing was a long shot, but worth the try.

Pickett hung up her cell and also sipped her iced tea.

"Robin is about ten minutes out," Pickett said. "She wants

us to order her normal for her if she isn't here by the time the waitress comes back."

Sarge nodded. Frighteningly enough, the three of them had normal meals they ate regularly when working a case like this. He wondered if that had anything to do with their age or if it was just what he had always done. He honestly had no memory of that, but if he had to guess, he would guess it was set-in-our-ways age.

"So," Sarge said, smiling at the wonderful woman beside him, "We have made a lot of headway to go nowhere real."

"We solved all the missing person's cold cases," Pickett said. "That's something. Might be a record for the most cases closed at once. And we know they are all alive."

"But alive where?" Sarge asked.

"I'm betting right here," Pickett said, shrugging, "all married or getting married, setting up husbands number eighteen."

They sat for a moment in silence, then Pickett said, "You think at some point we might move in together?"

Sarge laughed and looked at the woman he had fallen in love with.

"So why did this topic come up now?"

"Just thinking of those five women rushing into marriage," Pickett said, "for clearly the wrong reason, whatever it may be, and that got me wondering about our two condos and our situation."

"You want an honest answer or my safe answer," Sarge asked, smiling.

She laughed. "I want both. First the safe answer."

Sarge nodded. "Safe answer would be I think given time I would hope it would happen."

"Honest answer now," Pickett said.

"I would love to move in with you or you move in with me tomorrow. And besides, the kids would love it as well."

He was surprised that he didn't feel the slightest bit worried about admitting that to her.

She smiled and leaned over and kissed him. "I agree. And I had a thought if we can get the building management to sign off."

"Listening," he said.

"We put in an archway with pocket doors between our two places," she said. "We can leave the doors open most of the time, but if we have guests, we can close the door and let them use my place. And if we ever have to sell one place or the other, we just close it back up."

"Oh, god," Sarge said, smiling. "We're going to have guests all the time."

"So you like the idea?" Pickett asked.

"I like it a lot," Sarge said.

"Like what?" Robin said, sliding into the booth across from Sarge and next to Pickett. Neither of them had seen her coming across the restaurant.

"Some condo ideas," Pickett said. "We'll tell you later."

At that moment the waitress also appeared and took their orders for lunch. After she left, Robin said, "I have some news."

Sarge was stunned at that. Even though they were moving fast on this case, it felt to him as if they had hit the spot where the case would go cold again.

"What?" Pickett asked.

"We found who these sisters were originally," Robin said.

She opened a notebook and started reading. "We got a hit on the DNA from a distant family member and were able to track to the five sisters. Their original name was Jones."

"Jones?" Sarge asked, trying not to laugh. "Five women who change their names every year were originally Jones?"

Robin nodded. "Our March woman is the oldest at forty. Her original name was Beverly Jones. Then there were two sets of twins, not identical. So they are all within three years of the same age."

"Wow," Pickett said.

"Here is what gets interesting," Robin said. "When Beverly was fourteen, their father killed their mother. Seems he had been beating on the mother and the girls for years. Finally went too far."

Sarge felt his stomach twist. Now they were getting a glimpse of maybe why these women didn't stay with their husbands, but from all of the reports, the husbands were good men.

"What happened to the girls?" Pickett asked.

"Father went to jail, died there a year later in a knife fight," Robin said. "The girls were split up and put into foster care since they had no real other family that could deal with five kids."

"Oh, shit," Pickett said.

Sarge felt the same way.

Robin just nodded. "Five abused sisters split apart and put into a child care system. What possibly could go wrong with that?"

Sarge just shook his head.

"Beverly kept them all in touch," Robins said, "and together as much as possible, from the reports we found. When the last set of twins aged out, the five girls vanished. They never talked to even distant family members again."

The three of them sat there in silence for a moment, the sounds of the restaurant and the distant casino background noise.

The five sisters had lived through a nightmare made worse by no relatives being able to take them in. They had stuck together to get through it, which made sense to Sarge. But so many other things still made no sense at all.

Finally Sarge asked. "So why would that background, that history, that tragedy, make these women marry and then leave a husband, seemingly good husbands, every year?"

Neither Pickett nor Robin had an answer for that question.

The more they learned about all this, the more puzzling it became.

CHAPTER TWENTY-ONE

November 17th, 2016
Las Vegas, Nevada

They ate lunch while bouncing questions around about the motives of the five sisters, finding none at all that made any sense to Pickett. What had happened to those young girls, the horror they had survived, would certainly scare anyone.

And it made sense they were still very tight and had disappeared from any contact with a family that had allowed that horror to continue. But vanishing every year from good spouses just made no sense.

As they were just finishing their meals, Sarge's phone rang and he answered it. After a moment he said, "Hi, Mike. Any luck?"

As Sarge spoke and Pickett and Robin watched, Sarge got out his small notebook from his shirt pocket and started to write.

Pickett wanted to lean over and see what he was writing, but instead just sat there.

Finally, Sarge said, "Thanks, Mike. We owe you."

Mike must have said something because Sarge laughed before hanging up.

"Mike was able to get into the hotel servers and cloud storage," Sarge said, "but you didn't hear me say that."

Both other cops nodded and smiled. This would have been another matter if they were all still officially on the force, but they were just mostly private citizens who could bend rules far more than regular detectives could do.

"He said the hotel doesn't record exact connections or things like that, but they store usage from each room and basic levels for three years."

"Makes sense for lawsuit reasons," Robin said.

Sarge nodded. "Mike said he couldn't dig out specific addresses or anything like that," Sarge said, "but the activity from that room showed all five were online most of each day on the five computers. He said their activity looked like they were searching all sorts of databases."

"Searching for what?" Robin asked a half second before Pickett could ask the same question.

"Mike was wondering the same thing," Sarge said, shaking his head.

They sat there for a moment. Pickett knew they needed to get focused again. Somehow.

"Okay," Pickett said. "We have solved a bunch of missing person cold cases."

"And a few active ones," Sarge said.

"So we could quit right now," Pickett said, "get this to one of the active duty detectives and get him to get it in the papers to flush out the five women."

She hated that idea, but she wanted to float it to Sarge and Robin. Both of them were shaking their heads.

"So why are we not calling this one closed?" Pickett asked. "For me it is a gut sense that something bigger is going on."

"Agree," Sarge said, nodding.

"Completely," Robin said.

"So," Pickett said, "we need to change this focus to a conspiracy focus. We don't know the crime, but we know something is happening."

Both Sarge and Robin nodded.

The part that was bothering Pickett the most was that these women actually hadn't committed any real crime. At least that they could find.

"So," Sarge said, "with that focus, what about tracing how those fake ids and backgrounds are done."

"Will has two people on that," Robin said, nodding. "It bothers him that these five sisters could have such perfect and deep backgrounds for fake names year after year. That takes work, time, and preparation and it is driving Will nuts."

Pickett was very glad to hear that. When Will got focused, he found things that no one else seemed to be able to find.

"Good," Sarge said. "So everything keeps twisting around to their motive for pulling these vanishing acts."

"We have three theories," Pickett said. "Cover for a crime is the first. A lack of ability to commit to one relationship is second. A giant game is third. And the more I learn about these women, the more I think the first one is the only logical conclusion."

Again, both Sarge and Robin agreed.

The sounds of the distant casino filled the quiet in the booth. Finally Pickett asked, "Anyone got any ideas?"

Sarge nodded. "It's a long shot, but I think we get permission from the active detectives to tell Rich Hunter and Buddy

Charles who his wife really was, her background, what happened to her, what she was doing."

Pickett stared at Sarge. "You think them knowing who she was and her background might put a puzzle piece into this mess?"

Sarge smiled. "As I said, it's a long shot, but damned if I can think of anything else to do this afternoon."

Pickett could only nod to that because she didn't have any better idea either.

CHAPTER TWENTY-TWO

November 17th, 2016
Las Vegas, Nevada

Robin left to go back to help Will on his searches. Sarge and Pickett got their iced teas refilled and stayed in the booth, working together on a piece of key lime pie. From there they called Detectives Bower and Guy and told them what they had discovered so far and asked them to keep quiet on it for the moment, since they were working something bigger. They asked for permission to go talk with the two husbands again.

Both detectives agreed, as Sarge knew they would.

Pickett called Rich Hunter and he was surprised, but agreed to once again meet them in his office in forty minutes.

Buddy Charles said he would be open at 4 p.m. which gave them more than two hours to talk with Rich.

Sarge had no doubt at all that this would prove pointless and difficult to say to both husbands. But someone had to do it, so they might as well be the ones giving the news to the two men they had talked to.

Pickett paid the bill and thirty minutes later Sarge held the heavy door of the old office building on campus open for her.

"Always a gentleman," she said, smiling at him.

"Old school," he said.

She smiled at him. "We'll see how old later tonight."

All he could do was smile and hope he didn't blush at where his imagination went immediately.

Rich Hunter was behind his desk when they got to his open door. He signaled they should come in and have a seat and close the door, which Sarge did.

"So twice in two days," Rich said, "after all these years. Have you discovered what happened to Sandy?"

"We have," Pickett said.

Rich actually sat forward, stunned at that. "You know what happened to her? Is she dead?"

"No," Sarge said, "she is very much alive."

With that Rich sat back in his chair, the look of shock on his face clear.

Sarge figured the only way to get this out clearly was to start from the beginning.

"Sandy's real name was Beverly Jones," Sarge said. "She is the oldest of five sisters from back east. From the best we can figure, she was married three times before she met you, staying in each relationship about one year."

Rich started to object and Sarge held up his hand to stop him.

"We know how insane this sounds, but hear us out," Sarge said. "From 1998 to this year, Beverly Jones married and then vanished seventeen times. Her four sisters did the same thing."

Rich was shaking his head slowly from side to side.

"The five sisters grew up in a very abusive home," Pickett said. "When Beverly was fourteen, their father basically beat their mother to death. Beverly held the sisters together while they were all in foster care until they all vanished without a trace when the youngest two turned eighteen. Two years later in 1998 they started their vanishing routine here in Las Vegas."

"But why?" Rich asked, his voice not much more than a whisper. "She didn't take anything from me. Nothing. The police checked and we didn't have much to take as it was."

"Why is what we are trying to figure out," Pickett said.

Sarge just watched Rich's reaction. It was as he had suspected it would be. Stunned. Sarge had no doubt anger would come soon enough.

"Did Beverly, I mean Sandy say anything about children's homes?" Sarge asked. "Or about abusive relationships, sisters, anything that you can remember?"

"No," Rich said, shaking his head slowly. "She seemed so happy. Never said anything about sisters or abusive men or anything. She didn't even seem to mind my cousin Karl who treated his wife like shit. It didn't seem to bother her the few times we were around him."

"What happened to Karl?" Pickett asked a fraction of a second before Sarge could.

"Died just after Sandy vanished," Rich said. "But I was so focused on finding Sandy, I didn't even bother to go to the funeral."

Sarge glanced at Pickett, then asked Rich, "How did Karl die?"

"Food poisoning of some sort," Rich said, shrugging. "Or drank himself to death. I don't think anyone on the planet missed him, including his wife."

Pickett nodded.

Sarge wasn't sure what they had just discovered, but he had a hunch it might go deeper.

"Rich," Sarge said, "Other than your wife, can you please keep this to yourself for a few more days?"

"I can do that," Rich said, nodding. "You trying to figure out why she did this?"

"We are," Pickett said as she and Sarge stood.

Rich stood as well. "Is what she did to me and the other men illegal?"

"No," Sarge said. "But trust me, we will make her pay if we can."

Pickett reached out and shook Rich's hand. "Thanks for your help and sorry for the bad news."

"You figured out what happened to her," Rich said. "After this long, that's actually good news."

Sarge shook his hand as well. "Detective Bower will be in touch when it is all right to tell more people than your wife."

"Thank you," Rich said.

Sarge had a hunch that Buddy Charles, the next husband they planned on telling, wasn't going to take the news as well.

CHAPTER TWENTY-THREE

November 17th, 2016
Las Vegas, Nevada

When they got back to the car, Pickett called Robin, put the call on speakerphone, and told her about the abusive cousin dying right after Beverly vanished.

Robin said, "Holy shit. We'll get right on it."

And then hung up.

Pickett and Sarge both laughed.

"I love it when she does that," Pickett said. "Means she is excited."

Pickett knew that was going to be a tough search, through eighty-five husbands' extended families to find abusive men. But there was no doubt Robin and Will and his people could do it and do it quickly.

As Pickett headed them to Buddy Charles' office, she couldn't help but think that maybe, just maybe they had found the reason behind all of this.

They had just pulled up into the parking lot of Buddy's store and main office complex when Robin called back.

Pickett put it on speakerphone and Robin instantly started talking.

"Every husband's family we have checked so far, and that's twenty, had an abusive male die right after the fake wife disappeared. All of them, in one form or another, from food poisoning. Ten of them actually died in the hotel the woman vanished into."

"No one put any of this together?" Sarge asked.

Pickett felt the same sort of shock that Sarge had in his voice.

"Seems there was no need to," Robin said. "No one before us put these women together to see this kind of pattern, remember."

Pickett nodded on that.

"Think we need to talk with Buddy?" Sarge asked.

"Not yet," Robin said. "Head for home and I'll call you in an hour or so when we get the full picture in place."

"Oh, thank god," Sarge said.

Pickett laughed. "Yeah, not looking forward to this conversation."

And she hadn't been. She wanted to leave that to the active detectives on the case.

"When you cancel, tell him we are making progress and we'll be in touch," Robin said. "And I'll call you in an hour or so."

With that she hung up.

"Looks like we might have caught a break," Sarge said.

Pickett could only agree with that. She listened while Sarge thanked Buddy Charles for making time for them but they had to chase a lead and would be back with him as soon as things worked out.

Then Pickett got them through the later afternoon traffic and into her parking spot at the Ogden. On the way they had both decided they needed a little exercise, so they met fifteen minutes later in the condo's exercise room. No one else was there and they both did thirty minutes of running and weights before heading back upstairs for showers.

They were in Sarge's condo, feeding all three kittens their evening treat together when Robin called back.

Again Pickett put the phone on speaker.

"Every husband had an abusive family member that died right after the disappearance of the wife," Robin said. "All of them, no exceptions, and all from a form of food poisoning or alcohol poisoning."

"Any of them found to be an actual poison?"

"One doctor thinks that two of the men were killed purposely and both cases remain open as possible murders," Robin said. "In both cases both men showed up at the hospital in cabs, extremely sick and died within days without regaining consciousness. Cab drivers said the men were picked up at two of the hotels our women disappear into."

Pickett was shocked.

Could this actually be possible? Could these five sisters be serial killers and damn good ones.

"How long after the women disappeared," Sarge asked, "were the two possible murders committed?"

"One was six days," Robin said. "One was eight days."

"Any idea what the poison was?" Pickett asked.

"The doctor on the two cases think it was Croton Oil." Robin said. "It is used in animal lab testing in pain experiments and can be made from seeds of the Croton Tigium plant that grows in this area of the country."

"Mimics food poisoning?" Sarge asked.

"Almost impossible to spot and only takes ten to twenty drops to be fatal," Robin said. "You can add it to drinks or food and it takes about fifteen minutes for the reaction to hit once the poison is ingested."

"So they don't need a lot of it," Pickett said.

"Exactly," Robin said. "If what I have learned is right, the five women have killed eighty-five abusive men."

"Revenge for what their father did to their mother," Sarge said.

Pickett agreed completely.

"We now have a motive and a crime," Pickett said. "But no way to prove any of it and no idea where the women are now."

"Yeah, there's that," Robin said.

"Well, this is progress," Sarge said.

Pickett nodded. It was movement forward and smack into another dead end.

"You two enjoy your evening. Will and I are going to have date night. And no, don't ask."

With that Robin hung up.

Pickett laughed and at that moment the three kittens all ran into the living room together. Kittens seemed to never do anything slow.

And they were sure a wonderful distraction from the ugliness of the world.

PART FIVE

Still Another Dead Hand

CHAPTER TWENTY-FOUR

November 20th, 2016
Las Vegas, Nevada

Sarge was about as discouraged as he got on a case. For three days they had covered everything they could think of.

Nothing.

No headway at all.

As more and more information about the deaths came in, there was little doubt the men they were targeting were abusers. Clearly the five sisters did their research, which was more than likely what they were doing in those retreat hotel rooms.

And they did their research by marrying into a family to get the inside information about the abuser. Very careful as to their targets.

And from what Pickett and Sarge could figure talking to husbands, the sisters did it without much attention. For every husband they had talked to in three days, it was clear that at one point or another the sisters met each victim.

Today, Sarge and Pickett and Robin had all decided on trying to figure out how the sisters got the poison into the abuser's drinks or food.

It was a wonderful Sunday in late November, just four days before Thanksgiving, and Sarge wondered if he and Pickett had even needed the light jackets they wore on their walk to the Golden Nugget buffet. The sun was low, but had some warmth to it and the air felt like it might actually warm up.

Sunday in Vegas was like most other days in Vegas to Sarge. Neither he nor Pickett were religious, and besides, as a detective, cases didn't follow weekend rules, which had been part of the problem with his marriage.

Actually, the only way anyone who didn't work a regular five-day-a-week job in Vegas could tell any difference was that on Friday and Saturday nights there were a few more people than other nights. And on Sunday morning people in the casinos were either hung over or desperate to try their luck one more time before climbing on their plane home.

And most of them were dragging luggage around.

The buffet wasn't even half full and no family or hungover gamblers were near Sarge and Pickett's normal table when they got there. Robin hadn't arrived yet, so they got coffee ordered for all three and put their jackets at the table and headed to get food.

Robin arrived ten minutes later and within fifteen minutes all three of them were eating.

Sarge hadn't realized just how hungry he was this morning. He and Pickett had stayed up late watching a Mission Impossible movie. Nothing like watching a movie with fresh popcorn, three kittens, and the woman he loved to make a perfect Saturday night.

"Notebooks," Robin said as she finished her slice of ham and pulled out her spiral notebook.

Sarge took out his small pocket notebook and put it beside his plate, then went back to finishing his second waffle. Robin's call for notebooks meant they needed to talk about the case.

"I don't know if it's going to help us at all on this," Robin said, "but we need to focus on how the poison is being delivered. So I have all eighty-five case files of each death."

She took out of her pack a pile of gray folders and set them on an open area on the table.

To Sarge, the files were small. He was used to murder files and only two of these were even being investigated as possible murders. Those two files were on top and were the thickest. The rest were thin.

Very thin. Just unusual deaths in hotels or from food poisoning of undetermined origin.

The folders were so thin that Robin could pick all of them together out of her pack without a problem.

"I did a bunch of research on Croton Oil," Robin said. "It's frighteningly quick and lethal. It has to be ingested to do any real harm. And it causes extreme pain, so much so that the victims tend to drop into comas before eventually dying."

"So they have no time to talk," Pickett said, which was exactly what Sarge had been thinking.

"No time," Robin said, nodding.

"How hard would it be to get?" Pickett asked.

Robin shrugged. "Not difficult in enough quantity to kill this many men. A small jar would do it and the stuff isn't regulated."

"Oh," Pickett said, scratching something off her notebook.

"So connections in the deaths to the three hotels the women use?" Sarge asked.

"Half of the men were found dead in the three hotels,"

Robin said. "Another dozen or so managed to get either into cabs or to hospitals before collapsing. Cab records show they all came from the three hotels."

"The rest?" Pickett asked.

Robin shrugged and pointed to the files. "No mention at all. Three collapsed on the sidewalk, the rest died in the hospital without any record of how they got there."

"So let's just assume all of them were poisoned in the three hotels," Sarge said. "Safe assumption?"

"Seems very safe," Robin said, nodding.

"And the women can get in and out of any room in the hotel at will," Pickett said. "So they vanish into the hotel, change identity, stay under a fake name in another room until the target gets brought to the hotel and then manage to get the target poisoned, usually in a room."

"This has to be simple," Sarge said, sitting back and thinking about it. "Eighty-five times this has happened, so the method of getting the poison into the food has to be simple and not involve anyone else."

Both Pickett and Robin nodded, clearly also thinking.

Sarge then realized what he had said. "Not involve anyone else but the sisters."

Robin sat forward and started making notes.

"You thinking another sister lured each man into the hotel?" Pickett asked.

"They can't trust another person," Sarge said, "and the men need to get there in some fashion or another. How about in the two cases being looked at as a murder, any link to a woman?"

Robin slid him one file and Pickett another. In the file Sarge had, it was clear that there was no mention of anyone with the victim and the hotel room was under the victim's name.

"Witness in this one saw the victim with a woman in the hotel," Pickett said. "Short, in good shape, long blonde hair."

"Short," Sarge said, nodding.

"Robin," "Pickett said, "any chance we can get security video of this man and the woman entering the hotel?"

"We can," Robin said, nodding, gabbing her phone. "I'll get someone on it with facial recognition. But I am betting Sarge is right on this."

"So am I," Pickett said.

Sarge just smiled as Robin talked to someone in Will's office, then hung up.

"We'll know in fifteen minutes," Robin said.

Sarge wasn't so sure it was going to get them any closer to the five sisters, but in three days it was the first forward progress they had made and that felt great.

CHAPTER TWENTY-FIVE

November 20th, 2016
Las Vegas, Nevada

Around them the buffet sounds were quieting down as more and more of the morning breakfast crowd left. Now it was mostly just the sounds coming from the kitchen area that echoed over the large space. Pickett really felt comfortable here and she liked how the staff mostly just left them alone to take care of themselves, except to swoop past to pick up dirty plates and refill coffee.

Pickett felt slightly excited that they had had a breakthrough. It wasn't confirmed yet, but she was sure that Sarge was right and that the sisters helped each other.

And it made sense that there would be two of them in case something went wrong. After all, they were luring abusive men into hotel rooms to be alone. It wouldn't have surprised Pickett if a third sister was also in the return air ducts waiting to help.

"So if another of the sisters in disguise help get the man into the hotel room," Sarge said, "that brings us back to how in the world are they getting these disguises and identifications?"

That question had bothered Pickett a great deal.

Robin nodded. "Will asked the same question again last night. He has had no luck at all with the answer. These women set up complete fake histories and they manage to get driver's licenses and birth certificates. Very, very professional and all the identification and fake history holds up to a pretty good background check."

"Any sign they take the id from someone else?" Pickett asked.

"No," Robin said. "They make these new identities up out of whole cloth."

"How?" Sarge asked. "If they are going under fake identities into these hotels with the men, those have to be solid ids in case something goes wrong. So they could be coming up with upwards of ten completely new identities every year for the last seventeen years."

"Patterns in the identities?" Pickett asked.

Robin nodded and wrote in her notebook. "Might be worth a shot at running a computer program over the fake identities we know to see if there are repeating patterns of backgrounds, jobs, hometowns, and so on."

"And money?" Sarge said. "None of this can be cheap and they seem to take nothing from their husbands."

Money was something Pickett hadn't thought of at all.

"Damn," Robin said, looking up. "Each identity had to open a bank account of some sort and transfer money or write a check. That might be a link."

Pickett watched as Robin went back to quickly writing in her notebook.

Sarge excused himself to go get some dessert and Pickett asked him to bring her a piece of cherry pie if there was any.

Robin kept writing and Pickett just sat thinking. There had to be a way into the covers that these five women had set up. Since it was November, the women were more than likely working on their next husbands, maybe getting married by now. More than likely the woman who had been Sandy Hunter was already married or close.

They had to figure out how to find these five women, even if at the moment they couldn't pin anything on them.

Suddenly Pickett realized what she had been thinking about. Marriage.

There were a lot of marriages in Las Vegas every year. Hundreds a day. But they had these women's sizes and general ages.

Sarge slid a piece of cherry pie in front of her and sat down with a piece of his own.

"Robin," Pickett said.

Robin glanced up at Pickett, looking suddenly worried. Pickett never just called her by name like that unless it was something important and Robin knew it.

"I know after the case a month ago, none of us want to think about marriage stuff," Pickett said.

Sarge had a piece of pie halfway to his mouth. He stopped and put the piece down on his plate.

"Somewhere right about now the January and March sister and maybe the May sister might be getting a marriage license."

Robin nodded, thinking. Then she said, "We have their ages. If we could get the files, we could sort for age."

"Mike can get us the files again," Sarge said.

Pickett nodded. It was Mike in the big tunnel case last month who had helped them find key evidence by hacking into the marriage license database.

"How were all of the women married before?" Pickett asked. "Chapels, churches, backyards?"

"Nothing at all in any of the files on that," Robin said. "But we can look that up easily since all the wedding licenses had to be filed after the ceremony to make the marriage valid. All that is public."

She wrote a quick note in her book, closed it, gathered up the files, and put them in her pack and stood. "Will and I have a ton of searches to do and he's going to want to bring in extra help on this. If they get married in chapels, the photos will be available."

At that moment her phone rang and she answered it. She nodded for a moment, then said, "Thank you."

She put her phone away and looked at Sarge and Pickett.

"The woman seen with the last victim from September going into the hotel was Miss March. She had on a brown-haired wig, had heels that made her seem taller, and wore dark glasses. But facial has it at a one hundred percent match."

"So she lured Miss September's victim into the hotel," Sarge said.

"And one of them poisoned him," Pickett said. She could feel her stomach twisting.

"We have got to find these women before January," Sarge said.

"We don't have them rounded up by early December," Robin said, "we go public with all this. Splash their photos over the news and papers. We'll lose them, but save five lives."

Pickett could only nod to that. She didn't want to have these women vanish. She wanted to arrest them.

Personally.

CHAPTER TWENTY-SIX

November 20th, 2016
Las Vegas, Nevada

After Robin left, Sarge called Mike Dans again and asked for the favor of hacking the marriage licenses. Sarge couldn't believe he was asking someone to break the law. He never would have done that as an actual detective, but retired now, sometimes small lapses over the line saved lives.

Mike agreed and then Sarge and Pickett finished their cherry pies and sipped on their coffee.

"Seems like we made a little progress again this morning," Pickett said.

"It does," Sarge said.

"But something is bothering you, isn't it?"

Sarge glanced at Pickett and smiled. He loved how she could already read him. Before meeting her, having someone be able to really see him would have bothered him something awful. But he really liked it with Pickett.

"I've just been worrying about the evidence," Sarge said. "Even if we track and find these women, it will be like catching an endangered trout. Catch and release."

Pickett nodded and sipped on her coffee as a waitress nearby worked on cleaning all the empty tables.

"I think as we work on finding these five women," Sarge said, "we also need to start building a real case against them."

"And how do we start that?" Pickett asked.

"The poison is one lead," Sarge said. "I had never even heard of Croton Oil before this case."

"Neither had I," Pickett said. "We could also get them on creating fake ids and polygamy to hold them. Those we might be able to prove."

Sarge agreed with that. His focus was the murders, but at least they had something they might be able to hold the sisters on. But both of those charges wouldn't hold them for long. Days, maybe. And then the sisters would vanish.

"Also they all took their diamond wedding or engagement rings," Pickett said. "The most recent ones we could hold on felony theft."

Sarge nodded to that. It would be enough to hold them for a time. But they had to prove conspiracy on at least one or two of the murders.

Somehow.

If they could find them first.

They headed back to the Ogden at a comfortable walk. Sarge was really enjoying the cool morning air and being with Pickett, but he just couldn't get his mind off of one element of this case.

The money.

Finally, he decided that he needed to talk about what he was thinking about.

"I'm bothered by the money on all this," Sarge said.

"So am I," Pickett said, smiling. "In fact, that was what I was thinking about."

Sarge laughed and squeezed her hand.

"So let me outline what has me the most worried on this about the money," Pickett said.

"Fire away," Sarge said. "I bet we're on the same track."

"The women leave everything behind," Pickett said. "They are going to need a brand new wardrobe, hairstyle, everything. And that's not cheap, let me tell you."

Sarge nodded. "I honestly hadn't thought of that. I was thinking about a new apartment, first and last month's rent, new furniture to look the part they were playing, and so on."

"And they would already have much of that set up ahead of leaving," Pickett said. "Not only are these women masters of disguises, but in banking and setting up fake bank identities as well."

"Cars," Sarge said. "The sisters are buying five cars a year as well."

"This is really adding up," Pickett said as they reached the ground floor of the Ogden building. "And over seventeen years, where is the money coming from?"

"We're missing something," Sarge said. "I can feel it but darned if I can put my finger on it. And it has to do with the money."

"How about we go up to the rooftop balcony in your place," Pickett said, "get a couple cups of fresh coffee and sit with our notebooks staring out over the city."

"A perfect way to spend a Sunday morning in my opinion," Sarge said.

And it was.

But in two hours and three cups of coffee, they made no progress at all. But Sarge didn't mind, actually. Sitting with Pickett and staring over the wonderful view was reward enough.

CHAPTER TWENTY-SEVEN

November 20th, 2016
Las Vegas, Nevada

Sarge made them a light sandwich for lunch and after lunch they decided they both needed some exercise. For Pickett, that was the best way to clear her brain.

So after forty minutes of weights and running, she was back in her shower when one thought sort of came at her out of the blue.

What happens if the sisters weren't the only ones?

Pickett quickly got dressed and headed over to Sarge's place. He was out of the shower, but still getting dressed. He looked up at her and smiled when she came into his bedroom.

Damn, he was the most handsome man she could ever imagine being in love with. His muscles were still toned, his hair a gray that made him look distinguished, and his smile when he looked at her told her just exactly how lucky she was.

"Had this really horrid thought," she said as Sarge went

back to putting on his shoes. "What happens if the sisters aren't the only ones doing this sort of thing?"

Sarge looked up at her, clearly shocked and a little puzzled.

"What are you thinking?"

"I honestly don't know," Pickett said. "As far as we can tell, these five sisters arrived in Vegas young and with no money."

"Perfect targets for every lowlife wanting to take advantage of them," Sarge said, nodding and going back to putting on his shoes.

"Exactly," Pickett said. "We're running into professional ids right from year one with these girls, lots of money from the start, no mistakes at all that we can find, and a perfect way of killing targets."

Sarge looked at her. "Hard to imagine five sisters right out of the foster system having that kind of skill set just a year or so later."

"Bingo," Pickett said, feeling excited. "These sisters were trained and sponsored and if they were trained, who else was trained with them or since and who did the training?"

"Damn, you were right," Sarge said, looking suddenly worried, "this is a really horrid thought."

"We're dealing with professionals here, just as with the tunnel case," Pickett said.

She grabbed her cell phone out of her pocket. "I'll call Robin and Will, you warn Mike Dans to be careful with the marriage licenses."

Sarge moved quickly to the dresser and grabbed his cell phone as Pickett headed toward the kitchen with hers.

Their three kittens were all sleeping on the couch in the sun in the living room. Nose was on the back of the couch, Pete and Ree were stretched out on the cushions. Pickett knew those three kittens belonged together, just as she and Sarge did.

Robin answered and before she could say more than a word, Pickett told Robin what she and Sarge had come up with.

"Shit, shit, shit," Robin said when Pickett finished and hung up.

Pickett smiled at the phone and put it on the counter as Sarge came out of the bedroom.

"Mike hadn't gone in yet and will be cautious," Sarge said.

"Robin swore at me and hung up," Pickett said, laughing.

"I think you just kicked a hornet's nest here," Sarge said.

"Yeah, maybe so," Pickett said.

Sarge glanced over at the three sleeping kittens, then back at her. "You up for a nap before we head out.

Pickett smiled. "I would love that."

Sarge took her hand and they headed back into his bedroom to curl up together on his large bed.

Both of them had their cell phones with them. Even on a lazy Sunday afternoon, they were still detectives.

CHAPTER TWENTY-EIGHT

November 20th, 2016
Las Vegas, Nevada

Thirty minutes later it was Pickett's cell phone that woke them up.

"Yeah," Pickett said.

Sarge stretched and tried to listen. He couldn't hear a thing.

Finally Picket said, "Hang on, I'm putting you on speaker-phone. Tell us again what you just said."

She sat up on the edge of the bed and put her phone on the bed between them.

"Okay," Robin said as Pickett clicked on the speaker. "There is some pretty sophisticated tracking going on with each of the sister's last three names. Will and I are both pretty sure we didn't trigger anything and we have backed off completely now until we can work under the tracking."

"Tracking?" Pickett asked a half second before Sarge could.

"They are monitoring any kind of investigation into the

sisters' driver's licenses, missing person reports, and so on. Anything under that name is being watched. Including the two open possible murder cases."

"Wow," Sarge said, sitting up on the bed and putting a few pillows behind his back against the headboard. He was now completely awake.

"You check into Strickland?" Pickett asked. "He's done an investigation on Buddy Charles' wife."

Robin laughed. "Henry isn't going to like this, but his systems were bugged. The downloads only happen from his system once a week and we managed to get in and block the next download."

"You want us to tell him," Sarge asked.

"Yeah," Pickett said, "but not in his office. It might be bugged as well. We can find no trace of any, but I would rather have him looking than us."

"These people are that sophisticated?" Pickett asked.

"They are and this approach has answered a lot of questions for Will," Robin said. "This is a well-funded operation which explains the money and the high level of fake backgrounds and ids."

Sarge just shook his head on that. How could this even be? And why? Why would anyone fund this sort of thing?

"We've expanded our search to other abusers who were killed," Robin said. "You would be amazed at how many cases of food poisoning are reported in Las Vegas every year."

"Not sure I want to know that," Sarge said, laughing.

"Considering how many millions of meals that are served in restaurants every day in this city," Robin said, "the chances are very, very slim of anyone having a problem."

"But it happens enough to cover up these murders," Pickett said.

"It does," Robin said. "And often these men who are targeted have other underlying health issues, mostly diabetes, bad hearts, or alcoholism, so often that is written down as a cause of death."

"Logical," Sarge said. He couldn't even begin to remember the numbers of dead body calls he got over the years. When a person was found dead, alone in a hotel room, it was always considered a crime scene until other causes were determined. And that meant a detective had to look at the scene. Many of the scenes and bodies had not been pretty.

"We're being very careful now with the searches," Robin said. "We're looking for the same pattern now with missing persons and men with records of abuse suddenly dying."

"We'll go talk with Strickland," Pickett said.

Robin laughed. "Have fun with that. Back with you when we have more."

Then she hung up.

Sarge looked at Pickett who had also moved to sit up on the edge of the big bed.

"What the hell have we stumbled into now?" Pickett asked, shaking her head.

"My guess would be a major vigilante operation," Sarge said. "More than likely, just as with the sisters, all for revenge."

Pickett nodded.

They sat there on the bed in silence, thinking.

Sarge knew that both of them had seen their fair share of women beaten by their husbands. And a few instances of men being beaten and killed by their wives. Nothing good ever came out of such crimes.

Sarge believed that the abusers should be punished and given help for their problems. And at times he had remembered walking into a scene that was so brutal he actually wanted to just pull out his gun and shoot the abuser.

But he never had and never would.

These women might be picking victims that were, on the surface, bad people. But it did not excuse serial murder.

Nothing did.

CHAPTER TWENTY-NINE

November 20th, 2016
Las Vegas, Nevada

Henry Strickland was stunned that they called him on a Sunday afternoon, but he agreed to meet them outside his office in thirty minutes.

Pickett splashed some water on her face and then got a bottle of water for her and for Sarge out of his fridge. The three kittens had moved from the couch to spots along the window, still in the sun. Like most cats, they didn't notice that she and Sarge left.

The Sunday afternoon traffic was light and the day had never really gotten warm, although the sky was a deep, rich blue.

The drive was easy and when they got to Strickland's office, Sarge got out and moved to the back seat as Strickland came out and climbed in the front.

"So I'm assuming there is a reason for meeting in the car and not in there," Strickland said as he closed the door.

"We're afraid your office might be bugged," Sarge said.

Strickland actually laughed at that. "Not a chance in hell."

That was exactly the reaction Pickett expected him to have.

"Your computer system was bugged," Pickett said. "Robin and Will found it and got it stopped from its weekly download of your files."

Strickland opened his mouth and then closed it again. Then he asked, clearly anger in his voice, "Why and how did you know to even look?"

Pickett held up her hand for him to stop.

"Robin will send you the information about the bug," Pickett said. "Beyond my level. The reason is because of your case investigating Buddy Charles' wife."

"The five sisters are that sophisticated?" Strickland asked.

"No," Sarge said. "We don't think so. We think there is an organization, a sponsor of some sort that has trained them and been behind them for the last seventeen years."

"Oh, shit," Strickland said.

"That's why the incredible new identities," Pickett said, "and where all the money it would cost a sister to set up a new life every year came from."

"Got any idea who?" Strickland asked, shaking his head.

"Nothing yet," Sarge said. "These people are good, really good. We may never find them."

"But we are worried that they may be backing more vigilantes than just the sisters," Pickett said.

"So check your office," Sarge said. "Carefully. These people are damned good, as we said. Maybe have Mike come in and help you with the check to be sure. He's got all the best equipment to make sure everything is clear."

Strickland nodded. "I'll call Mike at once. From out here."

Pickett liked the private detective. He was rolling with this and doing what needed to be done.

"So what can I do to help?" Strickland asked.

"First off," Pickett said, "you call Mike and get him on the way, then call Robin and she and Will can explain the bug in your computer system and how it worked."

Strickland nodded.

"Then after you feel you are completely clean," Pickett said, "we could use your help searching your files for other cases that could be vigilante. Bad people getting what seemed to be coming to them. Or missing person cases that seem to make sense if looked at from this angle."

"You'll need to do it alone," Sarge said. "On a closed system. Have Mike help you set that up."

"I will," Strickland said. "Thank you for this. I owe you both one. I'll call if I find even a whiff of strangeness. I want to catch these bastards just for the chance of punching one of them in the face for hacking my system."

Pickett and Sarge both laughed as Strickland got out and moved over to the sidewalk in front of his office to call Mike.

Sarge got out and climbed into the front seat, then said simply, in his cold, calm voice, "Pull away from here, get out of sight and stop and park."

Pickett looked at him, feeling stunned, but did as he said as Sarge pulled out his phone.

"Robin," Sarge said. "Are you guys good enough to find out who Strickland is talking to right now on his cell phone? Or who he just called in the last minute or so?"

Sarge nodded. "Just a gut sense is all. And check that bug that was in his system. How long had it been there?"

Sarge nodded as Pickett pulled the car over in front of an empty lot and parked it.

"I hope I am wrong about this," Sarge said as he clicked his phone onto speaker.

"Shit, shit, shit!!" Robin said a few second later. "That bug was in his system for over ten years."

"Afraid of that," Sarge said. "It wasn't a bug, just an easy way to report in."

And Will's voice came in from the back. "You are never going to believe who Strickland just called. James Newell."

Pickett felt her stomach clamp up and Sarge's eyes were round.

"You're sure?" Pickett asked softly.

"Completely sure," Will's voice said from the background.

"He's calling Mike now," Robin said.

"We told him to," Pickett said. "So he's going to have to do that."

"After he is done with the call to Mike, let me know," Sarge said. "I'll call Mike, tell him what is happening."

"And we'll dig for a history of abuse in James' family," Robin said.

"Check his computer files that you got from the bug," Sarge said. "I'm betting buried in that there are files on all five sisters and maybe others doing similar things."

"Will do," Robin said. "I'll call you when Strickland is off the phone with Mike." Then she hung up.

Sarge pocketed his phone.

Pickett just sat there, feeling stunned. Finally she turned to Sarge.

"What tipped you to Strickland?"

"Coincidence at first," Sarge said. "He's had his firm for exactly seventeen years."

Pickett nodded. "I saw that as well."

"His tone when you told him there was a bug in his system," Sarge said. "He wasn't angry about the bug being there, he was angry at Will and Robin for getting into his system and finding it. He covered quickly, but that shocked him."

Pickett nodded. "I thought his reaction was as I expected. I only heard the anger, not what it was directed at. Great spot."

"Also," Sarge said, "when we told him about the five sisters, he was stunned we knew that, not surprised at the information."

"Missed all of that," Pickett said, shaking her head. "And it's obvious now that you point it out."

"That's why the three of us are partners," Sarge said. "We all see different things. But sure sorry to have James involved with this."

"There would have to be a reason," Pickett said. "So not going to believe it until we find that reason."

Sarge nodded and said nothing.

She sure hoped in her heart that Strickland calling James would turn out to be something else. Anything else.

But her detective gut told her it wouldn't.

PART SIX

The Big Play

CHAPTER THIRTY

November 20th, 2016
Las Vegas, Nevada

Pickett decided to move them away from Strickland's office so Sarge suggested they head to the Bellagio for Sunday dinner.

Robin called Sarge back as Pickett got them headed down the Strip. "Strickland is off the phone with Mike."

Sarge said, "Thanks."

This was going to be tough to explain to Mike, but he had to do it and do it quickly.

Mike picked up on the first ring. "Sarge, what can I do for you?"

"When are you meeting Strickland?"

"Tomorrow morning in his office," Mike said. "He wants me to check for bugs and set up an area of his office with a secure work station."

"Yeah," Sarge said, "we told him to call you and ask for just that. But there is a major problem. We are pretty sure Strickland is one of the people behind a long string of murders."

"Oh, great," Mike said.

Sarge could almost see Mike just shaking his head.

"I owe you dinner," Sarge said. "You got time for dinner and a long, complicated story involving five sisters?"

"Bellagio?" Mike asked.

"We're already headed there," Sarge said.

"See you in fifteen," Mike said and hung up.

Sarge nodded to Pickett. "He's on his way."

At that moment Pickett's phone rang and she handed it to Sarge.

He put it on speaker and said, "We're here and on our way to meet Mike for dinner."

"Bellagio?" Robin asked.

"Where else?" Pickett said, laughing.

"Wish I could join you, but I think I need to stay right here at my computer," Robin said. "The reason I called is that we found some ugly history in James' family."

"Oh, no," Pickett said softly.

Robin went on. "James' father abused his mother and his sister. His sister killed herself when she was thirteen. A year later his father was caught raping a twelve-year-old girl and arrested. He was killed in jail by another inmate."

"Oh, no," Pickett said.

Sarge felt sick to his stomach. He knew how much both Pickett and Robin liked James. This was going to be difficult at best for both of them. Right now Pickett was focusing on the road and traffic around her, but her jaw was set and her face pale.

"James' mother died while he was away in college," Robin said. "Causes unknown."

Only the traffic noise cut through the silence in the car. Sarge just felt sick to his stomach. He couldn't imagine how Pickett was feeling.

"We're looking into Strickland's family history," Robin said. "Just thought you would want to know about James."

With that she hung up.

Sarge looked at Pickett who was just shaking her head as she drove.

After a moment she said softly, "How could Robin and I have not seen this?"

"He helped you with cases, didn't he?" Sarge asked.

Pickett nodded.

"I bet his wife doesn't even know, and as far as James is concerned, he's just protecting the innocent like no one protected his sister."

"He thinks he's actually helping people?"

"He does," Sarge said. "But my worry is back to how are we going to prove any of this? We have lots and lots of circumstantial evidence that would get this case tossed out of court in a heartbeat. Especially if we accused someone with the reputation and money that James has."

"And we still don't know where the five sisters are," Pickett said as she pulled into the Bellagio parking lot.

"And if there are more killers besides the five sisters out there setting up their targets right now," Sarge said.

Actually, that was what worried him the most. Every day this took them to solve, the more chance someone was going to die.

CHAPTER THIRTY-ONE

November 20th, 2016
Las Vegas, Nevada

Pickett wanted to just hit something. She and Robin had trusted James, maybe more than they should have at times. But he had been a good friend, a generous donor to charities, and seemingly a good citizen of Las Vegas.

Now they were thinking about him for the money and brains behind a serial killing spree. This couldn't be right. But having Strickland call him right after they had that conversation was very damning.

And his background didn't help the reasonable doubt either. But as Sarge said, they had no real case. They had a lot of suspicions and connections, but no evidence.

So she needed to believe in James for the moment and not completely hang him without evidence.

And as careful as Strickland and the five sisters were, and maybe James as well, they might never find actual evidence.

Pickett and Sarge walked in silence on a sidewalk beside the parking lot and into the Bellagio Casino. The late afternoon air had a chill to it and inside the door of the casino the sounds of people laughing and talking and bells ringing grounded Pickett a little more.

She took Sarge's hand as they headed along the wide tile walkway toward the café.

As they got to the entrance of the café, she looked up at Sarge. "Really glad you are here with me on this one."

He smiled and squeezed her hand. "I'm glad to be anywhere with you."

She laughed. "Wow, a fast and perfect answer."

She kissed him.

He just laughed and said, "The truth is always a good answer."

"In this case, yes," Pickett said, laughing.

And laughing made her feel better. Still angry, but at least thinking again.

Amazingly, their regular booth was open back among the plants and they gave the woman who seated them their drink order of two coffees and glasses of water.

The booth had a large oak-colored table and leather seats and plants ringed the back of it giving it a sense of privacy. The noise was louder in the restaurant than normal, mostly because it was the dinner rush. And there were a lot of tourists walking by along the front of the café pulling suitcases.

Mike seemed to appear out of nowhere as they were getting settled.

He was a solid man, all muscle, with wide shoulders and close-cropped hair. He was former Special Forces but never talked about his background. He had intense eyes that never seemed to miss a detail, yet a smile that could relax anyone around him. He was also one of the smartest people Pickett had ever met, and that was going some.

Pickett had liked him from the moment she had met him a month earlier. Robin and Will thought he was the best there was in the business at security and finding things. And the team of former Special Forces men he had working for him were amazing.

Mike gave the waitress his drink order when she brought the water and coffee and they all ordered dinner at that point as well, since they all knew the menu so well.

Mike had a rare top sirloin with a baker, Sarge had a chef's salad, which was huge, and Pickett decided she wanted halibut with a dinner salad.

Mike then took out his notebook and pen and asked, "What the hell is going on?"

Starting from the beginning, they told Mike about the case, the five sisters, their discussion with the husbands, the poisoning of the abusive men in the hotels, and so on.

When he got to how many men they thought had been killed, he just shook his head and kept writing.

Then Sarge told him about the conversation with Strickland, his reactions, and how Will and Robin had traced the fact that he had called James Newell the moment they had left, before calling Mike.

"The James Newell?" Mike asked, clearly shocked. "The architect, the same one you went to for help with the older hotels?"

Pickett nodded. She then filled Mike in on what Robin had found about James' background.

Mike sat back, thinking as the dinners arrived. They all started to eat in silence until Mike said, "So you think Newell is the money behind all this and Strickland the general in the field?"

"Pretty much," Sarge said. "And we don't have a damn bit of evidence on any of it that we can prove. So we could be completely wrong."

"I'm still hoping we're wrong about James Newell being involved in some way," Pickett said. "But my gut tells me we aren't."

"A friend?" Mike asked.

Pickett nodded. That was all she felt safe doing at that moment. She focused on her halibut, knowing it tasted good, but not being able to really enjoy it.

"So at the moment only the three of us and Robin and Will have this entire picture?" Mike asked.

Pickett and Sarge both nodded.

The three of them ate in silence until finally Mike said, "How do you two get into this kind of stuff?"

Sarge laughed lightly. "We've been asking ourselves that same question."

"But the problem is that we can't really prove what we have found," Pickett said. "We can't confirm any of it."

"And for all we know," Sarge said, "there are more killers out there besides the five sisters."

That thought made Pickett push away the rest of her dinner.

"We need to prove this, Mike," Sarge said. "Somehow."

Mike nodded.

"And if we can't prove it enough to put anyone in jail," Pickett said. "We have to at least stop it."

Sarge and Mike nodded.

And Pickett knew that they both wouldn't feel satisfied with that result.

She wouldn't either.

CHAPTER THIRTY-TWO

November 20th, 2016
Las Vegas, Nevada

They finished their meals and were drinking coffee, still helping Mike fill in what gaps they could, when Sarge came back to the question he had been asking all along.

"We need to follow the money," Sarge said.

He knew that was one of the major keys on this. And now, if the money led back to Newell, as they suspected it did, that would help.

Mike sat forward. "What are you thinking?"

"These five sisters must start lives over every year," Sarge said. "That has to be expensive."

"Just new wardrobes of clothes that don't look all new would take time and money to put together," Pickett said. "And they all buy at some point under the new name a car and rent an apartment and furnish it. Not cheap."

"We have the women's names and details for seventeen

years," Sarge said. "There has to be a money trail to each of them from somewhere."

"And the marriage license information you wanted me to get is to see if a couple of the women are applying for new marriage licenses?" Mike asked.

"If we can just spot one of them," Sarge said, "we might have it easier to track."

"But you said these women are setting up the next target family before they leave the one they are with. Right?" Mike asked.

"So right now all five of them are spending money for yet a new life," Pickett said.

"You think any of this information is going to be on Strickland's computer?" Mike asked.

"I don't think so," Sarge said. "Even with the bug reporting device on there, I can't imagine Strickland being that careless."

"Neither can I," Pickett said. "And if Newell is involved in this, I know he never would let anything get to him either."

Sarge sat back. He couldn't believe what he was thinking, but it was the only answer that made sense on all of this.

"They have a headquarters," Sarge said.

Pickett looked at him, frowning.

Mike slowly nodded.

"More than likely a store front," Sarge said, "a perfectly normal legit business of some sort, that everything concerning the sisters and maybe other killers, goes through."

"A charity," Pickett said.

Sarge knew she was right. He was about to suggest that she call Robin, but Pickett already had her phone to her ear.

"Makes sense," Mike said, nodding. "And that would give Strickland and Newell and who knows who else cover."

"Robin," Pickett said after a moment, "Sarge thinks there

might be a headquarters for all this, some legit business or charity to give Newell and Strickland and others cover."

Pickett nodded. Then she clicked off her phone and set it on the table next to her coffee.

"Robin and Will and their people," Pickett said, "of which they have five working right now, are going to see if there are any patterns in the five sisters' shopping habits and credit card purchases."

"So back to the murders for a moment," Mike said. "You think one of the women lures an abuser into the hotel and the other is waiting there with Croton Oil to poison the guy. Right?"

"Croton Oil is tough to detect if not looked for," Pickett said. "And it mimics food poisoning right up to the point the victim falls into a coma and dies."

"Takes about fifteen minutes to work," Sarge said, "which would give the women time to escape, yet that is a short enough time that the victim would never be able to figure out what happened and talk."

"Every victim we have traced," Pickett said, "has died alone in a hotel room or from food poisoning or something related to a health condition that could have been triggered by Croton Oil."

Sarge had a hunch Mike was going somewhere with this line of questioning, so he just waited.

Mike nodded to all this, then asked, "So the theory is that these women marry these men to get into the family and do research?"

"That's the theory," Sarge said. "They are very careful and each victim we have looked closely at has been an abuser, of that there is no doubt."

Mike nodded. "So my guess is that in those retreats the sisters take, they are researching families of men they have met.

If no abuser in the family, they don't bother to get to know the man better."

Sarge nodded. "And doing it from a remote location in a hotel room would make sure that nothing about the search could be traced later."

"Exactly," Mike said.

At that moment Pickett's cell rang.

She picked it up and said, "You want this on speaker?"

Sarge watched as Pickett glanced around. "Booth area is clear. I'll warn you if someone is approaching."

With that Pickett put the phone on speaker and set the phone in the middle of the table between them.

"Women's thrift store," Robin said, "out near the old Boulder Highway. Sells used clothing and furniture and donates to a number of women's shelters around the city."

Sarge nodded. That would make sense and explain part of how the sisters got new/used clothes every time they had to restart a life.

"The store has existed for seventeen years," Robin said.

"Could have guessed that," Pickett said.

Mike nodded.

"Every incarnation of the five sisters that we have traced so far has spent money in that store," Robin said.

"Still no proof," Sarge said.

"James Newell is a major donor to the store," Robin said. "Right from the beginning."

"Damn it," Pickett said, softly.

"And Strickland does regular work for them," Robin said. "Also right from the beginning."

"Okay," Sarge said, leaning back and looking around to make sure no one was listening. "Lots of coincidences there."

"Mike," Robin said, "Will and I can only dig so far."

"I'll get myself and a few others on it tonight," Mike said.

"Thank you," Robin said. "We found a few alarms along the way, but nothing you won't be able to get past if you need to. For a small thrift store, they have a very sophisticated computer system."

Sarge sat forward on that. "More sophisticated than would be needed to run just five sisters in what we have learned?"

"Far more," Robin said.

"Shit," Mike said.

Sarge could only agree with that.

CHAPTER THIRTY-THREE

November 20th, 2016
Las Vegas, Nevada

Pickett felt like they were making progress and with Robin and Will and all their computer people on the trail, and tonight Mike and his people would dig even deeper, they might be able to actually get to the bottom of all this.

But she was honestly worried about where the bottom of this cesspool of murder actually was. And how many people were swimming in it.

The sun had long set by the time they left the Bellagio. The air had a sharp bite to it and a slight wind from the north made it feel even colder.

After Pickett got her car started and actually turned on the heat, she suggested to Sarge that they take a drive out along the old Boulder Highway, not to stop at the thrift store, but to just take a look at it.

Sarge agreed. Both of them wanted a look at what they

might be facing. More than likely they would never have to even go in the place, but it still felt right to go look.

She got onto Flamingo and headed east until she ran into the Boulder Highway and then turned right.

The old Boulder Highway had, at one time, been the main road out of Las Vegas, heading up to the town of Boulder. But a faster freeway had left the old highway with scattered nineteen-fifties' hotels, warehouses, and empty lots where businesses used to exist.

The thrift store occupied what had been a small market at one point and looked to be pretty good sized. It sat on a large lot with a cracked and old parking lot completely around it. Two of the dozen parking lot lights still worked, but only barely.

Pickett didn't slow as she drove past, then went four more blocks and turned around in an old Burger King parking lot and headed back.

As they passed the thrift store the second time, Sarge said simply, "I'm betting there's something under that parking lot."

Pickett could see what he meant. The land was far, far bigger and the parking lot far larger than was needed for even an old market, let alone a thrift store. There had been no reason to ever pave it all.

He took out his phone and called Robin, putting it on speaker as Pickett headed them back into downtown and toward the Ogden which she could see towering next to the casinos ahead.

"Robin," Sarge said. "We just did a drive-by of the thrift store. Any old plans or permits for a large basement under that store and the parking lot around it?"

"Didn't see any," Robin said. "But didn't look that closely at the history yet."

"Also check the power bill for that place," Pickett said, realizing what she had seen without noticing it. The power line running to that building was much larger than needed.

Sarge nodded.

"We'll check on both and call you back," Robin said.

"What do you think might be under there?" Pickett asked. "If anything?"

"With this case," Sarge said, "I would be afraid to even take a guess."

Pickett laughed at that. "I'm hoping for evidence."

"Yeah," Sarge said. "We can only hope. But not holding my breath. These people have been far too smart for far too long."

"And dangerous as well," Pickett said.

Sarge only nodded at that.

Once she parked in her spot in the underground parking garage of the Ogden and they were walking toward the elevator, she asked, "Up for a movie?"

"I would love one," he said, smiling at her. "Try to take my mind off of this case."

"I might be able to help with that after the movie as well," Pickett said, smiling at the man she was in love with.

"If we're still awake by then," he said.

"Oh, wow," she said, pretending to frown as they got into the elevator. "You sure know how to give a girl a complex."

He laughed and kissed her as they rode up the elevator to the penthouse level.

They had almost made it to his bedroom with Sarge doing his best to make sure she didn't have a complex, as she said, when Robin called them back.

"Complex interruptus," he said, laughing as she took out her phone and they moved into the kitchen.

"On speaker," Pickett said, putting the phone on the counter. "We're in Sarge's kitchen."

"Good spot on the basement of the thrift store," Robin said. "It's the size of a large warehouse down there. And the entire place pulls a lot of power at times."

"Printers and computer levels of power?" Pickett asked.

"Even more at times," Robin said. "Will thinks that's where they make the fake ids, but that wouldn't take that kind of power or space. Something else is going on in that basement."

"Maybe Mike will find out what?" Sarge said.

"We hope so," Robin said. "Will and I have dug about as far as we dare dig without warrants and we have not one shred of evidence to even try to get a warrant."

Pickett nodded.

"We understand that," Sarge said.

"Make sure your alarms are on tonight," Robin said. "We kicked a hornet's nest today and we have no idea how they might respond."

"Copy that," Pickett said. "You two have a good night. See you at breakfast?"

"I'll be there," Robin said.

"Breakfast is here tomorrow morning," Sarge said. "These people use poison as a normal way of killing. We take no chances."

Pickett stared at Sarge for a moment, then nodded.

"See you for breakfast at your place then," Robin said after a moment. "Gives me a chance to see the kittens again."

With that she hung up.

"Well that was a mood killer," Pickett said, shaking her head as she clicked off her phone.

"I'll make the popcorn," Sarge said.

"I'll go get changed," Pickett said.

"And I'll feed the kittens their snack. You know that Nose has already moved in here."

Sarge pointed to the couch where Nose, Pete, and Ree all were sound asleep on the couch together.

Pickett laughed. "She's just a little ahead of me is all."

"Not by much, I hope."

Pickett kissed Sarge. "Not by much, I promise."

She headed for the door to go to her place to get changed. She loved the idea Sarge had of knocking an archway between the two condos. Maybe, as soon as they got this case finished, they would do that.

All they had to do was find some evidence.

Maybe she would move in before the case wrapped up, since real evidence was something they were in very short supply of at the moment.

Very short, as in none at all.

CHAPTER THIRTY-FOUR

November 21st, 2016
Las Vegas, Nevada

Sarge was enjoying cooking breakfast for Pickett and Robin. Both of them had offered to help, but he had told them they could help by keeping the kittens entertained and refilling his coffee when it got low.

He managed to actually get them some ham and cheese omelets that looked pretty good, a small slice of ham, and toast and get it all out almost at the same time.

They all went to the table upstairs that showed the late-fall morning out over Las Vegas. It looked a little cold and gray and cloudy, but the view made up for anything like that.

"I keep forgetting how spectacular the view is from up here," Robin said as she put out a pitcher of orange juice and a coffee pot.

Sarge had just put all three of their plates on the table and

Pickett was bringing up the coffee cups and a pot of coffee for refills.

"It really is stunning," Pickett said.

"I can't imagine ever getting used to it," Sarge said. And he couldn't. It seemed fresh every time he came up to this level.

Earlier in the month he and Pickett came up here on warm evenings and just sat with a glass of wine on the balcony and talked and stared at the view of the city. He was already looking forward to the spring when the weather would allow them for a time to do that again.

"So Will's people didn't find much more last night," Robin said after they all settled in to eat. "On the surface that thrift shop does some fantastic charity work for women's issues around town."

"On the surface?" Pickett asked right before Sarge could.

"Nothing we can find other than that," Robin said. "And no reason at all for that basement."

They talked while they ate and at one point had a great laugh at all three kittens chasing each other up the stairs, around them, and then back down. Sarge could not tell which kitten was doing the chasing. They seemed to take turns all in mid-stride.

They had just started into their coffee when Sarge's phone rang. He knew from the number it was Mike.

"Any luck?" Sarge asked as he clicked on the phone.

"More than expected," Mike said. "You guys at the Nugget?"

"My place," Sarge said. "All three of us."

"I'm ten minutes out," Mike said. "I need to tell you three some of this in person."

He hung up and Sarge put the phone back in his shirt pocket and looked at the concerned faces of Pickett and Robin. "Mike's on his way with news."

Both nodded and all three of them stood and gathered up the dishes and headed down to the kitchen. They had breakfast cleaned up and the dishwasher going as Mike rang the bell.

Sarge poured him a cup of coffee and they all four went back upstairs to talk.

"Wow," Mike said, looking around at the view. "This can't be beat."

"That I agree," Sarge said.

"So here's the news," Mike said. "That basement is a sanctuary for abused women."

Sarge sat back. That was not at all what he was expecting.

"In fact," Mike said, "It's one of three in the city for women and there is one for men as well, completely hidden, and part of a nationwide underground-railroad type of operation."

Robin looked at Mike. "So they get women and kids new ids, money, a new place to live, and get them out of town and away from abusive husbands?"

"Exactly," Mike said. "Each sanctuary has family living centers, counselors, and a hospital area for injuries."

Sarge kept shaking his head. He knew there were women's shelters around town, but in all his years as a cop he had never heard of anything like this.

Pickett seemed as stunned as he felt.

"Women from other cities are coming into Las Vegas," Mike said, "with new lives and abused women from here are sent to other places."

"This sounds amazing," Robin said.

"So if these five sisters have this sort of resource," Pickett said, "why are they killing abusive men instead of just rescuing the women and kids?"

"Some women don't want to be rescued," Sarge said, softly,

remembering more than he wanted to remember of beat-up women who refused to press charges against their husbands.

All three of the others nodded. They had all seen it far, far too often. And far, far too often the women and sometimes the children ended up dead in short order.

They all sat silent for a moment, then Mike said, "There is no doubt that both Strickland and Newell are connected to this women's shelter. Both are part of a fairly large donor network and Strickland does work for the shelter when needed. More than likely helping them set up safe homes for the women and families coming in here in Las Vegas."

"So we have a network of underground shelters doing great work," Robin said, "and five serial killer sisters that might or might not be linked to the shelter in some way."

Pickett nodded.

Mike just sort of looked pained.

"And if they are linked to the shelter or the deaths," Sarge said, "we still are sitting here without a lick of evidence to prove any of it."

"I feel almost dirty now even trying," Pickett said.

Sarge could only nod to that. He had no idea what they should do next except keep on trying to find the killers, if the women were the killers, and hope they weren't connected to the shelters in any way.

He had a hunch they were connected, but not in any way that could be proven.

And he was convinced that all the good people working at the shelter would know nothing about the five sisters killing abusive men.

This case had just become a no-win case.

And he hated that.

PART SEVEN

Freezeout...The End Game

CHAPTER THIRTY-FIVE

November 21st, 2016
Las Vegas, Nevada

Pickett hated with a passion how this case had turned. Over the years as a detective, she had always liked cases that were more black and white, good versus bad, cops versus murderers.

This case was so far from black and white, she didn't know what to do. Even though she couldn't prove it in any way, she knew she had five sisters who had killed at least eighty-five men.

The fact that the men were abusive husbands didn't matter. They were human beings and the sisters had choices other than cold-blooded murder.

But now there was a chance the sisters were tied into a person she considered a good friend, James Newell, and also a women's shelter that clearly did the work of saints in helping protect women and families.

But they had no proof on that either.

All speculations.

And not even Mike, with all his computer specialty work, could make any link at all with Newell, Strickland, the five sisters, or the women's shelter under the thrift store.

"So we're at a dead end," Sarge said.

The four of them were still sitting at the table in his loft, the fantastic view of the city around them.

Robin and Mike nodded.

"I hate this," Pickett said. "There has to be some way we can tie those sisters to at least one murder without dragging down the shelter at the same time."

"That's what we work on then," Robin said.

Sarge nodded. "And we have to find the sisters and stop them before they kill again, remember."

Pickett agreed to that. It seemed at this point that was all they could do.

Mike left to get back to work and Pickett and Sarge and Robin sat staring into space, trying to figure out what to do next.

Pickett had not one idea.

Not one.

"Facial recognition," Sarge said. "Possible to develop a program that would scan for faces from grocery stores, drug stores, traffic cams, places like that?"

Robin nodded. "Long shot and a lot of data. But we might get lucky and find one of them."

"And if we find a sister," Pickett asked, "then what?"

As she expected, neither Sarge nor Robin had an answer to that one. But she knew they had to try.

"So what else can we do on this fine Monday?" Pickett asked.

"I have to go shopping," Sarge said, smiling. "I was hoping I could cook a turkey dinner on Thursday for you two and Will and maybe a few others from the Cold Poker Gang who didn't have anywhere to go."

Pickett looked stunned. "Didn't know you could cook a turkey dinner."

"Used to all the time," he said. "But the last few years just went out. But this year, if you two would like, I can give it another try."

Pickett smiled and kissed him. "I would love that."

And she would. It sounded wonderful.

"Count me and Will in as well," Robin said.

At that moment Robin's phone rang. She glanced at the phone and Pickett watched Robin's face go white.

"It's James," Robin said.

"Well," Sarge said, "we did kick his nest a little yesterday."

Pickett felt as surprised as Robin looked.

Robin clicked on the phone and said, "Hi, James. Can I put you on speaker? Pickett and Sarge are here as well."

She nodded and clicked on the speaker and put the phone down on the table between them.

"Hi, James," Pickett said.

"Robin, Pickett, Sarge, great talking with you again," James said.

Pickett was surprised that his voice sounded perfectly normal and not in the slightest bit stressed.

"What can we do for you, James?" Robin asked.

"Actually," James said, "It's what I can do for you. I know you three have been looking into a special thrift store out on the Boulder Highway. Thought you might want a tour."

"We would love one," Robin said. "Very kind of you."

Robin's eyes were round and Pickett was as surprised as Robin was looking.

Sarge just sat there shaking his head.

"I can be there in about one hour," James said, "if you three are free."

"We are," Robin said.

"See you then," James said.

Robin clicked off the phone and then just stared at it.

"What just happened there?"

"He seems to know everything we are doing," Sarge said.

Sarge picked up the phone and hit a call number. After a moment Sarge said, "Mike, need your help in two areas."

Sarge nodded.

"We just got a call from Newell offering to show us the shelter in one hour."

"Back-up would be fantastic, thanks," Sarge said after a moment. "And could you sweep my condo and Pickett's condo for bugs? Newell seems to know what we are doing at any moment."

Sarge nodded. "Thanks."

Sarge hung up. "Mike and his people will have us covered completely if something happens in that shelter. He's going to meet us in thirty-five minutes at the Burger King down the road from the shelter and give us bugs and tracking pins that should work through any kind of blocks. Plus he'll track our phones."

Pickett nodded. "Really good thinking."

"I just wish I knew what the hell we were walking into," Robin said.

"Just don't touch or eat or drink anything," Sarge said, smiling.

"Not funny," Pickett said.

"Yeah," Robin said.

Sarge just chuckled.

Ten minutes later Pickett was pulling out of the underground garage and turning to head out the Boulder Highway. She had a hunch that one way or another, they were going to get some answers on all this very soon.

She just had no idea what the answers might be.

CHAPTER THIRTY-SIX

November 21st, 2016
Las Vegas, Nevada

Sarge made sure his tracking button was secure and well-hidden. And that his gun was loaded. He had no idea what they were walking into here, but considering they had no other real leads, this seemed to be the only solution.

Just under one hour from when they had said they would meet Newell, Pickett pulled her SUV into the driveway of the thrift store and parked in the parking area around back.

The lot was larger than it had looked from the street and if all of that was open underground, it would be huge. And there wasn't the slightest bit of evidence that anything existed under the old, cracked pavement.

The morning air still had a bite to it, but the day promised to be a nice one. As they were headed toward the front of the thrift shop, James Newell drove in.

He parked his white Cadillac four-door next to Pickett's

SUV and the three of them waited for him to get out and join them.

"Thanks for the tour," Robin said as he approached.

"I was expecting to give it the moment you two came out to my house," Newell said. He pointed around at the vast parking lot. "We're all pretty proud of the work we do here. And in other three sanctuaries like it around the city."

Sarge just nodded and neither Pickett nor Robin said a word.

Newell led them through the front door of the thrift shop and said "hi" to a woman working behind the counter. Sarge missed her name, but Newell pointed to the three of them.

"Three of Las Vegas' finest detectives."

The woman nodded, looked around to make sure no one else was in the shop and pushed a button.

A shelf with lots of junk kitchen items on the back wall swung open and Newell led the way in behind it.

A bright light came up behind the shelf and showed a clean and modern staircase heading down.

Pickett glanced at Sarge, clearly not happy that in less than a month two cases had taken them underground. Sarge had to admit he wasn't that happy about it either.

At the bottom of the stairs was a large metal door.

Newel punched in a code he didn't let them see into a lock box and the door swung open.

Beyond was a reception area that looked like a modern hospital reception area. It was bright, with modern furniture, and a smiling woman sitting behind the desk. A large screen television showed changing desert shots on one wall, giving the sense the room had windows.

The woman was thin, in her middle thirties, maybe, and

looked completely in shape. She had on a white blouse and dress slacks.

"Hi, James," the woman said, standing and coming around from behind the desk. "Thanks for giving us some warning on guests coming through. We have a couple new admissions that we needed to clear from the public areas to help them feel safe."

"Completely understand," James said. "Thanks for allowing this tour. These are three detective friends of mine from the Las Vegas force. They can be trusted without fail."

Sarge felt shocked at what James had just said and clearly Pickett and Robin felt the same way. The three of them had just spent a lot of time possibly endangering this entire enterprise. So clearly James was betting that when they saw the place, it might make them forget about eighty-five murders.

Sarge just shook his head. Not likely and James clearly wasn't a stupid man. He knew Pickett and Robin would never do that, so there had to be another reason for this tour.

Beyond the door behind the receptionist area, there was a large living area. All modern, all decorated with plants. Five or six seating areas with modern couches, chairs, and coffee tables filled the space. Everything was done in light tan, wood, and brown tones and to Sarge the place felt comfortable, and again gave no sense of being underground at all.

That was helped by the varying ceiling height through the place. One area would have tall ceilings, another area the ceilings were down lower for a more intimate feel.

Clearly James had done some designing on this and it had worked.

Across the way was what looked to be a community kitchen with three or four different-sized dining tables.

And past that was a large playground, with slides and all the modern stuff for kids to play on.

There was no one to be seen.

Sarge glanced around. The receptionist had not come with them, but the door still stood slightly ajar behind them.

"Wow," Robin said.

"This is stunning and very comfortable," Pickett said.

Sarge had to agree with both of them.

The hallways leading off in three directions," James said, pointing at the three, "are to family apartments. Each apartment has a full living room, kitchen, dining area, and bedrooms. All fully furnished. Groceries are delivered every day for what each woman or family needs and asks for."

"All secured?" Sarge asked.

"Completely," James said. "But we have never had an issue here because we are so careful in extracting the women from their situations. And everything is blocked completely down here, including the audio Mike Dans helped you into a little bit ago. However, we left your trackers on so Mike and his people wouldn't worry."

"Is Mike working for you?" Sarge asked.

James laughed. "Oh, heavens, no. But I respect him and admire him and his team and what he does."

"Sounds like you have a pretty good team of your own," Robin said.

"We do," James said, nodding. "It's required to keep these women safe and get them the professional counseling help they need to get restarted in life. Plus get them moved and into a new life."

Now Sarge had to admit he was impressed. But he figured it was time to lay all their cards on the table since it was clear James and his people had been far, far ahead of them all along.

"So what about the five Jones sisters?" Sarge asked.

"They vanished, it seems, within an hour of the two of you

showing up at my house," James said, smiling at Sarge and Pickett. "I had no doubt that the three of you would eventually find them. Eventually."

"And where are they now?" Pickett asked.

James just shook his head. "I honestly have no idea. I wish I did."

Sarge just stared at James for a moment. Pickett looked shocked.

James indicated they move to a table. "Let's sit down so I can tell you the entire story as I know it."

Sarge wasn't so sure he wanted to sit with this man, but he would at least give James some rope to hang himself.

CHAPTER THIRTY-SEVEN

November 21st, 2016
Las Vegas, Nevada

Pickett wasn't sure what she was the most stunned about. The fantastic and modern facility hidden under an old parking lot or the fact that a man she had trusted had just admitted knowing about five serial killers.

They all sat down at the table and Pickett sat back. She wasn't at all sure she wanted to hear this story. But she was willing to listen, to see if they could find any path to real evidence.

"First off," James said, "I want to tell you how pleased I am that you three managed to take this as far as you have."

"Sounds sort of condescending," Robin said.

Pickett felt the same way.

"It was not intended that way," James said, looking worried. "When I called Andor and suggested he give the three of you this case, this was exactly what I was hoping for. Exactly."

"You called Andor?" Sarge said a half second before Pickett could.

James nodded. "I only learned about the five sisters about two months ago and I was appalled to say the least. Shocked and disgusted and yet I had no evidence at all to go to anyone about what was happening."

Sarge waved his hands in the air and said, "Let's just stop right there. Would you start over from the beginning, back when you built and designed this place, and what it is all connected to?"

"And then work us to the sisters," Robin said.

James nodded and took a deep breath. "I am certain you have researched my family history and the abusive father I had."

Pickett nodded, as did the other two.

"When I started to attain a level of money, I started to look around for areas where I could help others and I came across these shelters. That was over twenty years ago and the shelters at that time were mostly just houses where women tried to protect abused women from their abusers."

Pickett knew all that. As a detective, she had been to her fair share of those homes on emergency calls as an abused wife tried to hide from an angry and usually drunk husband. In one case the angry husband had sprayed the building with gunfire, killing his own wife, kid, and one social worker.

"At that point in time," James said, "a national organization was forming, pulling in large private money to set up better facilities and networks to help the women and families relocate and get needed help, both physical and mental help. I joined the organization and helped design and set up the four clinics in this area."

"An operation of this size, to remain secret, takes some real work," Sarge said.

Pickett completely agreed with that. She couldn't even imagine the money this took.

"It takes money and good people," James said, nodding. "And everyone who works here is fully committed to the cause. They often work frighteningly long hours to help others."

"So could you now tell us about the five sisters," Robin said.

James nodded and actually looked embarrassed. "As I said, I discovered two months ago that there is a splinter off of the national organization, one that is not sponsored or condoned in any fashion, that backs what the sisters were doing."

"And what exactly were they doing," Sarge asked.

"They were looking for the abused women who would never leave the abuser no matter how bad it got. They searched for the women trapped completely in the abuse cycle."

"And then the sisters would take care of the abuser," Robin said.

"That's what I came to understand two months ago," James said, nodding.

Pickett had to admit, James looked sick and pale even admitting that much.

"I tried to find out who they were through the national organization and no one had any idea what I was even talking about. And honestly, I believed them. This organization has nothing to do with the one that funds this place and all the others around the country."

"Who tipped you to what was happening?" Pickett asked.

"Strickland," James said. "He's worked with us from the beginning, helped in so many ways without real pay. He got the one missing person's case, Kathy Charles, that you were investigating and went deeper and discovered the death of an abuser in the woman's family."

Pickett was impressed.

Robin nodded. "I knew he was good, just didn't know how good."

"He's amazingly good," James said. "But this drove him crazy all through the summer until he managed to put all the pieces together about the five sisters, in much the same way you three did in much faster time."

"And he brought you his findings two months ago?" Pickett asked.

James nodded. "I got so angry, I thought I was going to have a stroke."

"But neither you nor Strickland could find any evidence, could you?" Sarge asked. "Hold up in court evidence? Or even who was funding the sisters."

"Not a bit," James said. "So I called Andor and had him give you the Sandy Hunter missing person's case as a favor to me. And not say anything."

"Does Andor know what this is all about?"

"He doesn't have a clue," James said.

"So how do you know the sisters have vanished?" Robin asked.

"I called the organization's main office and told them that three detectives were investigating on the case and getting closer. Of course, the main organization claimed they had no idea what I was talking about or why I was even telling them."

Pickett nodded.

"Two days later Strickland told me that five cases of missing persons had been filed for five women, basically the five sisters. One was married, four had boyfriends. Strickland said it was the five sisters cutting and running. So I at least stopped five murders."

"That's what we were hoping to do as well," Pickett said.

"So why did you have Strickland play along instead of just coming clean with us?" Sarge asked.

"Because it has been my hope from the start that you would find these five sisters and find proof, real evidence, that they were serial killers and put them away without touching all this."

He waved his hand around at the massive room they were sitting in.

Pickett understood that.

"We know they are serial killers," Robin said.

"We know how they did it," Sarge said.

"And we know that they used Croton Oil to poison the men," Pickett said.

"But you have no proof at all, do you?" James asked, shaking his head. "Neither does Strickland."

"Not a bit beyond a little circumstantial," Sarge said. "The victims were all from families the women disappear from. One victim was seen with one woman on tape right before he died."

"Not a damn thing that would hold up in any court," Robin said. "I can tell you, it's driving Will and his people nuts as well."

"So now what do we do?" James asked.

Pickett sat back for a moment as silence filled the large space. Then she said simply, "We monitor. We combine forces and monitor."

The three looked at her like she had lost her mind.

"We have Strickland and his people," Pickett said, "we have Robin and Will and all their resources, Mike and all his resources, and we have your network here, James, nationally and all your resources. Right?"

James nodded.

"We set up searches to monitor for any known abusers suddenly dying of food poisoning. Anywhere in the country."

"Can we do that?" James asked, looking at Robin.

"We can," Robin said, nodding, clearly thinking. "But as Pickett said, we will need to combine forces. Maybe hire one or two people to work it all the time."

"I'll fund it," James said. "I feel like this has blemished all the good work we have done here in the last twenty years. I want to make up for that."

"You know," Sarge said, "chances are that we only drive these people like the sisters back into hiding every time."

"But just as we stopped five deaths here," James said, "every time we do that we can save lives. And after all, that's the point of this place."

Pickett liked that idea a lot. Usually, as a detective, you got to a scene after someone was dead. Doing this would save lives and with James' organization, help the victims of the abuse, on both sides, get help.

She liked that more than she wanted to admit.

EPILOGUE

November 24th, 2016
Las Vegas, Nevada

Sarge handed Pickett two large bowls of mashed potatoes to take upstairs to the table. And then handed Robin two bowls of stuffing.

"You realize there are only five of us," Robin said, shaking her head as she followed Pickett up the stairs.

Sarge didn't care that he had made enough food to feed twenty. He loved Thanksgiving and loved cooking and didn't realize how much he missed doing it until early this morning when he got up to put in the turkey, leaving Pickett curled up under the blankets looking beautiful.

Sarge just smiled at Robin's comment. He had invited Strickland and James and his wife Patty as well, which Pickett and Robin didn't know about. So it would end up eight for his first real Thanksgiving holiday with Pickett.

Eight friends together.

The condo smelled wonderful, with the cooking turkey and baking rolls. He had gotten a big enough turkey to make sure that he and Pickett had lots of leftovers.

He glanced around for a moment, letting the turkey cool just a little more before starting to cut it.

At the moment the three kittens were stretched out in the living room on the couch, ignoring all the food and talking. To them it was just another day.

But to Sarge this day felt special. It felt like the start of something new, a new family in a way.

Pickett was coming down the stairs when someone rang the bell.

"Can you get that?" Sarge asked Pickett. "I need to carve up this monster."

"You can smell that turkey two floors down," Mike said as Pickett opened the door. Behind him was James and Patty and Strickland.

Pickett just laughed and gave them all a hug, then offered to take their coats.

Robin came back downstairs, laughed, shook her head at Sarge and went to give them hugs as well.

Sarge had felt right having them all together for the holiday. After the tour of the sanctuary and the explanation, they had spent the last few days setting up details about their new monitoring project.

It was going to take some time to find the right people to staff it and get everything in place, but it would happen. And who knows how many lives it would save.

Sarge had little hope that any real evidence would be found to catch and put the women away, but if they kept finding them and stopping them from killing more, that would be enough for now, until the evidence did surface.

James had said that his people from the sanctuary had contacted in secret the five wives of the sister's recent targets and offered them help if needed. And James' people had set up secret monitoring in the homes to catch abuse there before it escalated into a murder.

Granted, they had not yet caught and convicted five women serial killers. But Sarge had hopes that over the years, with the monitoring program, they just might find them with evidence enough to convict them.

But on the original missing person case, the Chief of Police had been stunned that they had solved it and eighty-five total missing person cold cases at the same time.

That was a record, even for the Cold Poker Gang.

And on Tuesday night, the entire Cold Poker Gang had given the three of them a standing ovation. To Sarge, that had felt just amazing.

But it didn't beat how it felt right now, working to serve a Thanksgiving feast to some fantastic friends he hadn't even known a month ago.

And eating a wonderful holiday meal with the woman he had come to love.

The condo felt alive, felt like a home now. He would have never imagined that happening a month ago.

At that moment Pickett came into the kitchen and kissed him on the neck. "That was a wonderful surprise. Thank you."

"My pleasure," he said. "Now, as I carve the turkey, could you get the rolls out of the oven and into baskets and upstairs?"

"Gladly," Pickett said.

"But first," Sarge said, smiling at her, "tell me you love me before I go into battle with this monster beast."

"I love you," she said, laughing. "And tomorrow, let's go talk with the board about opening up that door between our places.

It's time we call both of these places our home, don't you think?"

"I like that idea more than you can know," he said, smiling.

She kissed him again.

"Now, he said, "don't let the rolls burn. We have eating to do."

"And drinking," she said.

"And then pie," he said. "Can't forget pie."

"Never," she said, laughing. "Never forget the pie."

The Cold Poker Gang Mysteries continue with the next book in the series, Ace High. Following is a sample chapter from that book.

PROLOGUE

April 3rd, 1991
Las Vegas, Nevada

The Landmark Hotel, or as it was called before it was closed, the New Landmark Hotel, felt more like an ancient ruin to Steven Bell. And as a long-time resident of Las Vegas, that made him sad. In its glory, the hotel and casino had really been something to see, towering proud and gleaming over the valley. Now it desperately needed paint, the windows hadn't been washed in years, and weathered plywood covered all the entrances. It just looked worn out and tired as only a well-used and not-maintained building could look in the desert winds and heat.

Sad, just flat sad, that a building of such importance to an entire city had been left to rot.

He just hoped someone with a lot of money would come in and bring the Landmark back up to use. Maybe not as a hotel, but as offices and restaurants or a something.

Anything.

But after seeing the inside of the place, he was starting to doubt if that would ever be possible no matter the amount of money.

The Landmark had been designed to imitate the Space Needle in Seattle, thirty stories of tower with restaurants and a show ballroom with a huge dance floor at the top. For the longest time it had been the tallest building in the valley.

Most of the rooms and suites were in the buildings around the casino area on the ground floors, but some suites lined the sides of the tower all the way to the top.

Construction on the place had started in the early sixties, but it wasn't until Howard Hughes bought the Landmark that it opened in 1969. The hotel and casino went through numbers of owners after that, never really getting profitable until finally closing in August of 1990.

Clearly to Steven, no money had been spent at all to keep the place up in the last few years of its existence. Everything just looked worn or broken. The last guests before this place closed must have been disgusted at what they found. He would have been.

Now everything inside was to be liquidated and it was Steven and his crew's job to do an inventory. At first, when the court had hired him, he thought the job sad, but that thought vanished the moment he started through the place.

There just wasn't much worth selling left. Even worth selling or not, they had to inventory it.

Old blackjack and craps tables and such in the casino area might be worth something, but the casino had leased all its slots and those were long gone already. He and his crew of four found the beds in rooms were often rotted and the mattresses bug-infested. The wooden end tables and coffee tables in most rooms were worn and scarred. Lamps and their shades often were spotted with age or just broken.

All of the bar equipment was so dated as to be almost antique. And food had been left in the fridges and the pantries to rot when the place shuttered. If this place had sat like this in any other town but Vegas, the entire building would have been overrun by rats by now. As it was, he only saw some minor signs of mice. But who knew what was living in the walls.

He and the four people working for him had focused on the ground floor and casino area for the first few days. Now they were working their way up the tower slowly, leaving all the restaurant equipment and furniture in the top floors for last.

The afternoon of April 3rd was getting warm outside and the inside of the hotel was getting stuffy. He had already shed his outer shirt at lunch and was now in just a T-shirt and jeans. He had a work belt on his waist with most tools he would need including extra pens.

They had started at sunrise to avoid this kind of heat problem and in an hour they would call it a day. He couldn't even begin to imagine what this place would feel like without power and air conditioning in the summer. It would be like walking through an oven.

He was looking forward to getting home to his condo and showering off the smell of mold and rot.

He had climbed ahead of his crew to the twentieth floor, just doing a quick walk around the hall, making sure all doors were open as they should be.

Just as with every other floor, the carpet in the hallway was worn and everything smelled like it had been closed up far, far too long. The beam of his flashlight cut through the darkness of the hallway, with light coming in from the open suite doors to help some.

He stirred up a fine cloud of dust as he moved and the dust floated in the beam of his light. He desperately wanted to go throw open a few of the windows in the suites to get some fresh air in the place, but then they would just have to close them. Wasn't worth the effort to even try to pry open rusted and old windows.

Ahead of him the hallway was even darker because the door to Suite 2017 was closed. He moved to open it, but it was locked. He tried the pass-key, but that didn't work either. More than likely the door was jammed shut.

"Munro, bring the crowbars," Steven said into his radio. "Got a stuck door on twenty."

"On my way," Munro said.

Steven moved on around the rest of the suite hallway, making sure all other doors were open. They were. So far, he and his crew had been forced to pry open or break open about thirty doors. He was just happy it wasn't a lot more. These old casino doors were solid.

Munro met Steven at the closed door and handed him a large crowbar. Munro was the largest man on the crew. Young, and with a wife and two kids, he never missed a day and was the hardest worker Steven had ever met.

Steven also knew Munro worked out at a local gym every day after work and had muscles on top of muscles. But when it came to heavy lifting and forcing a closed door, Munro was the best.

The two of them quickly had the trim off the door and with both bars jammed between the frame and the door, they managed to shove the door inward.

"Shit," Munro said, stepping back as a wave of dry, rotted-smelling air hit them. "What the hell is that?"

Both of them moved back along the hallway and away from

the smell. Steven knew exactly what that smell was. Something had died in that room. He knew the smell of death from his days on search and rescue for the county. And it wasn't the smell of fresh death, but old death.

Steven took out a mask from his tool belt and handed an extra to Munro. "Let me take a look first, decide what we need to do."

Munro nodded. Even in the pale light of the hallway, Steven could see that Munro's face was white. He clearly had never dealt with anything dead before.

With masks on, they went back to the now-open door.

Steven took two steps inside and stopped. Munro stopped right beside him, looking over his shoulder.

It was clear what had caused the smell.

On the bed was a naked woman.

Dead, very dead.

"Shit," Munro said and turned away, going back into the hall to throw up what he had had for lunch.

Steven just stared.

The mummified body still looked very human in the daylight pouring in through the window. She had long brown hair spread out around her head and she looked peaceful, with her hands crossed over her chest as if someone had placed her there, looking up at the ceiling, legs together. She had been young and thin.

And she had clearly been dead for some time.

A blue backpack lay on the bed beside her and her clothes, what looked like a white blouse, a white bra, and jeans were draped over an old chair. He could see nothing at all that looked like a cause of death.

In fact, she looked very peaceful.

He backed out of the room, making sure to not touch anything.

Munro was leaning against a wall, trying to catch his breath. The hallway now smelled of old death and Munro's former lunch.

Steven said into his radio to his crew. "Mark clearly where you left off and everyone meet at the truck at once. Don't depend on remembering where you were. We're done for the day."

More than likely they were done for the week. Crime scenes tended to do that to jobs.

Steven then patted Munro on the shoulder and the two of them headed for the staircase.

The hotel had gotten even sadder now. Its last resident was a young dead woman.

NEWSLETTER SIGN-UP

Be the first to know!

Just sign up for the Dean Wesley Smith newsletter, and keep up with the latest news, releases and so much more—even the occasional giveaway.

So, what are you waiting for? To sign up go to deanwesleysmith.com.

But wait! There's more. Sign up for the WMG Publishing newsletter, too, and get the latest news and releases from all of the WMG authors and lines, including Kristine Kathryn Rusch, Kristine Grayson, Kris Nelscott, *Smith's Monthly, Pulphouse Fiction Magazine* and so much more.

To sign up go to wmgpublishing.com.

ABOUT THE AUTHOR

Considered one of the most prolific writers working in modern fiction, *USA Today* bestselling writer Dean Wesley Smith published almost two hundred novels in forty years, and hundreds and hundreds of short stories across many genres.

At the moment he produces novels in several major series, including the time travel Thunder Mountain novels set in the Old West, the galaxy-spanning Seeders Universe series, the urban fantasy Ghost of a Chance series, a superhero series starring Poker Boy, and a mystery series featuring the retired detectives of the Cold Poker Gang.

His monthly magazine, *Smith's Monthly*, which consists of only his own fiction, premiered in October 2013 and offers readers more than 70,000 words per issue, including a new and original novel every month.

During his career, Dean also wrote a couple dozen *Star Trek* novels, the only two original *Men in Black* novels, Spider-Man and X-Men novels, plus novels set in gaming and television worlds. Writing with his wife Kristine Kathryn Rusch under the name Kathryn Wesley, he wrote the novel for the NBC miniseries The Tenth Kingdom and other books for *Hallmark Hall of Fame* movies.

He wrote novels under dozens of pen names in the worlds of comic books and movies, including novelizations of almost a dozen films, from *The Final Fantasy* to *Steel* to *Rundown*.

Dean also worked as a fiction editor off and on, starting at Pulphouse Publishing, then at *VB Tech Journal*, then Pocket Books, and now at WMG Publishing, where he and Kristine Kathryn Rusch serve as series editors for the acclaimed *Fiction River* anthology series, which launched in 2013. In 2018, WMG Publishing Inc. launched the first issue of the reincarnated *Pulphouse Fiction Magazine*, with Dean reprising his role as editor.

For more information about Dean's books and ongoing projects, please visit his website at www.deanwesleysmith.com and sign up for his newsletter.

www.ingramcontent.com/pod-product-compliance
Lightning Source LLC
Chambersburg PA
CBHW010447100726
47904CB00008B/2512